# Hauntings from Wayne
## and Beyond...

*For Caleb,*
*Enjoy + believe!*
*Cathy Cook*

### By Cathy Cook

*Hauntings from Wayne and Beyond*
©2012 Cathy Cook
ISBN: 978-1-938883-18-7

All rights reserved. No part of this book may be reproduced in any form or by any electronic or mechanical means, including information storage and retrieval systems, without permission in writing from the author, except by a reviewer, who may quote brief passages in review.

Cover design by Daniel Bouthot

All photos by Cathy Cook unless credited otherwise

*Produced by*
Maine Authors Publishing
558 Main Street, Rockland, Maine 04841
www.maineauthorspublishing.com

Printed in the United States of America

*dedicated to
those who believe*

# Table of Contents

Introduction ............................................... 3
Preface .................................................... 4

*Chapter 1*
Neala Jennings Lives with Ghosts ........................ 7
*Chapter 2*
The Way House in Wayne ................................ 9
*Chapter 3*
Greentrees in Mount Vernon ............................ 17
*Chapter 4*
A Recollection by Hannah Faulkner..................... 31
*Chapter 5*
Full Moon of July ....................................... 33
*Chapter 6*
Stevenson's Brick Farmhouse ........................... 37
*Chapter 7*
Dave's Appliance Store and the Ketchen House .......... 41
*Chapter 8*
Judy and John's Hauntings .............................. 51
*Chapter 9*
The Old Nickerson Place in Readfield................... 59
*Chapter 10*
The Elvin Farm ......................................... 67
*Chapter 11*
Evelyn Potter Visit ..................................... 71
*Chapter 12*
Thunder Castle Hill..................................... 75
*Chapter 13*
The Mattie Hackett Story .............................. 81
*Chapter 14*
The Walton Farmhouse ................................ 85
*Chapter 15*
Sally Towns' Ghost Story ............................... 89
*Chapter 16*
The Old Cottage in Wayne.............................. 93
*Chapter 17*
Wayne UFO Stories .................................... 99
*Chapter 18*
The Underwood House ................................ 103
*Chapter 19*
The Old Stinchfield Place.............................. 111
*Chapter 20*
Cheryl Bennett Ladd Story ............................ 113

*Chapter 21*
The Wing Cemetery in Wayne.......................... 115

*Chapter 22*
Paul King Stories...................................... 117

*Chapter 23*
Camp Androscoggin Ghost Tale ...................... 121

*Chapter 24*
Mysterious Footsteps in Wayne....................... 123

*Chapter 25*
Three Pine Farm in Readfield ......................... 125

*Chapter 26*
Readfield Historical Society Visit ..................... 129

*Chapter 27*
Spirit Lady in Mount Vernon.......................... 133

*Chapter 28*
The Pelletier House in Fayette ........................ 135

*Chapter 29*
Leon Robert's Reincarnation Story..................... 147

*Chapter 30*
LeeAnn's Ghost Stories................................ 157

*Chapter 31*
Joan Stiehler's House in Wayne....................... 161

*Chapter 32*
The Oellers House in Winthrop ...................... 165

*Chapter 33*
The Kosma's Ghost Experiences....................... 173

*Chapter 34*
Monmouth Hauntings ............................... 179

*Chapter 35*
The King House in Monmouth....................... 183

*Chapter 36*
The Dragonfly Shop in Litchfield ..................... 187

*Chapter 37*
Annette's House in Temple ........................... 193

*Chapter 38*
Sleigh Bells in Farmington............................ 199

*Chapter 39*
Ghosts in New Sharon ............................... 203

*Chapter 40*
The Mill Agent's House in North Vassalboro............ 211

*Chapter 41*
The Androscoggin House in Wayne.................... 221

Acknowledgements ................................... 228

*We are not earthly beings having a spiritual experience;
we are spiritual beings having an earthly experience.*
—Teilhard de Chardin

# Introduction

*I find the idea of ghosts and spirits very comforting.
We are never really alone.*

My adventures with ghosts really began when I was a young girl. However, one day about three years ago during an inspired moment, I found myself saying to my writer friend, "Wouldn't it be fun to write a book about true ghost stories of this area?" Though I had heard about a few local hauntings, this statement just came off the top of my head.

My friend gave me some advice, and tools to tackle the project. I started to ask people if they had ghosts, and soon began the wonderful journey of collecting ghost stories. It's amazing how many people have experienced ghosts in their homes, and have rich stories to tell!

It has been a great adventure, visiting many beautiful and historic old homes, and meeting many amazing people. Sometimes my friend came along, and sometimes it was my daughter Jillian. Eventually, I met Annette and Paula, who are able to see and communicate with ghosts. I decided to invite them on many of the interviews. They were able to provide excellent insight about the ghosts and spirits that occupied those houses. I learned a lot about spirits and ghosts, and gained some knowledge about how the spirit world works.

Most of the stories were transcribed from actual recordings, and a few of the encounters were written by the storytellers themselves. Many of the people I interviewed led me to other people with stories to tell.

# Preface

Ghosts are not what you think. They are not scary, violent, or dangerous as the media sometimes portrays them. They are around us all the time, and occasionally try to make themselves known to us. I have come to believe this over many years, beginning as a child, and continuing with the stories I have collected here.

I believe that the stories in this book are an honest portrayal of what ghosts and spirits are really like. My hope is that the reader will not only be entertained, but will learn more about the spirit world.

So I thank you, dear readers, for keeping an open mind. Enjoy!

*photograph courtesy of Judy Danielson*

*Chapter 1*

# Neala Jennings Lives with Ghosts

*I came across this story written by Neala Jennings, a long-time resident of Wayne, and felt it would set the mood nicely for this book. Of course, I take ghosts even more literally than Neala did. This story appeared as an article in The Mainer, titled "Wanderings on the Wild Side," in March, 1995.*

Neala wrote,

"There are ghosts all around me. I haven't seen them, nor have I heard them, but I know they are there. Why else would I feel so welcomed when I walk into my house? Why else do the fields and surrounding woods beckon so, the ancient apple trees hold out their branches to me? There must be ghosts. You see, I live in an old house; old by central Maine standards, that is.

Early settlers found the spring down over the hill, and I suspect that's where they first settled, because the remains of an old cellar hole and a well are still faintly visible. They didn't stay there long, though; it's wet and boggy, so they moved up the hill and found a better location.

7

They built a barn, apparently in 1796, because we once found a board with that date carved into it. They also put up a log cabin, or so old Mr. Maxim used to tell my mother and grandmother. He still worked a woodlot nearby, and on cold winter days he'd leave his lunch bucket by our stove, to keep it from freezing. He had stories about these early settlers, his ancestors, and Mother later passed them along to me. The cabin had a central chimney, and in the front hall the old boards attest to the fact! They are pitted with holes left from burning embers.

One story had it that the father was left a widower with a large number of children. He or his eldest son (I never got this part straight) married and brought his young bride back to take care of this motherless household. The morning after her arrival, the bride had to get up and prepare breakfast for the family, with just the open fire for her stove. The number seventeen comes into the story, but I can't remember if that was the age of the bride or the number of children. How hard they must have worked with their horse and their brawn. Stone walls are everywhere around the fields my father reclaimed, and through the woods that once were fields.

My mother said that when she came here as a child, around 1910, you could clearly see the farms on the surrounding hills, and that all was fields and pasture between. Actually, a lot of it was orchards, because at that time they were still shipping barrels of apples, many of them overseas. Her stepsister once put a note in one of the barrels, and received an answer from someone in England! Work crews came through the area, going from farm to farm picking the apples. The women of the house prepared a huge noontime meal and gallons of tea or a cold drink for them. Mother mentioned root beer, which was home-brewed, and a molasses-based drink, probably switchel.

The barn has fallen down, but the stone walls are there, and the last few apple trees, hollow and gnarled, but still offering up their autumn beauty, their spring bouquet of bee-enticing blossoms, and their summer shade. The bluebirds returned a few years ago: how the old trees must have welcomed them!

I live with ghosts, you see; the bride stirring porridge in an iron kettle over that smoking fire, the farmer planting apple trees, old Mr. Maxim sitting by the stove reminiscing about the old days.

I live with ghosts, and I wouldn't have it any other way!"

*Chapter 2*

# The Way House in Wayne

*One of the first stories I collected was from an unlikely neighbor who is a well- known and respected interior designer from Florida. This elegant woman surprised me when she told me she had ghosts in her house. Here is her story.*

I am Fi, and my husband De and I bought the Bennett house in 1999. It is now 2009, so we have been here for about ten years. When we first moved into the house, which was built in 1830, we had to become accustomed to the slanted floors due to the years of settling. Naturally, we were told that a ghost had resided here. Frankly, we don't believe in ghosts.

However, we had a house guest who came and stayed in what is now the upstairs master bedroom. When she went to bed, she noticed that the latch on one of the old-fashioned closet doors was unlatched. However, when she woke up in the morning, it was latched. That got her a little curious, and she said, "Fi, I think you have a ghost in your house."

I said, "I'm sure we don't," and then she told me about the latch.

A couple of years later, De and I noticed that there was a thumping sound every so often. We decided that it was the wind blowing on the flag in the front of the house, and it sounded odd because we were in the front bedroom.

However, our daughter Wendy came and spent quite a bit of time in the house when we were not in residence. She called one day and said, "Mom what do you do about your ghost?"

"What ghost?"

"The little girl who lives here."

"Wendy, we don't have a little girl that lives there."

"Oh, yes you do, Mom, because she thumps up and down the stairs almost every night!"

We have heard her giggling at times. There was a time when a roommate of Wendy's was staying at the house, and she said, "I heard a little girl giggling."

Wendy said, "So did I!" Well, they stayed here for about two more weeks, and they heard a lot of strange noises and thumping and bumping.

Wendy's partner, Jan, said to me one time, "Do you know you can actually invite a ghost to leave? You just sit in the middle of a room and you say firmly and politely to this ghost that it should leave this residence."

So I thought I would try that. I felt a little foolish, sitting there by myself talking to a ghost, but I did. I said to the ghost, "We have a lot of people going in and out of here, and one more person is just a disturbance, so we would appreciate it very much if you would just leave. And, thank you very much for your attention, and we hope not to hear from you any time soon. Good night!"

I had heard through the grapevine that Wendy was again staying at her parent's home, and so I set up a time to meet with her and her partner, Jan. I wanted to hear their version of the hauntings they had experienced. Wendy and Jan have lived in California and New

York, but they decided to stay all winter at Wendy's parent's home in Wayne. Wendy is an actress, and Jan writes alternate-reality video games for a living. Though neither of them ever believed in ghosts before their visits here, they now definitely believe that ghosts exist! An intelligent and witty couple, they were dead serious about what they saw and heard at the house.

Jan began by telling me a story about their first experience staying there, about seven years ago. She and Wendy had just gotten a yellow lab puppy, Wally, and decided that Wayne, Maine was a better place to live with the puppy. So they came up to stay for a couple of months. Here is Jan's story:

When we first came here, we both started to smell cigar or cigarette smoke. It seemed like it would come all at once. Well, at first we thought it was coming from the neighbor's house or that perhaps some of the men who worked on this house were smoking cigarettes, and maybe had just arrived and were working downstairs. The smell was that strong. We always seemed to smell the smoke near the laundry room.

One night I said to Wendy, "Are the men working around here?" She asked why, and I mentioned that I had smelled the cigarette smoke again. She said that no, there hadn't been anybody working on the house that day. I thought it must have been blowing over from the neighbor's yard, and so I didn't say anything because I didn't know anything about ghosts at that time.

We have a lot of friends in California who believe in ghosts and reincarnation and all of this "woo woo" stuff, and we always thought it was just crap! I remember thinking, I am a "Mainer," and I don't believe in that kind of stuff!

We were getting ready to move back to New York in a couple of days, and one night we were getting ready to go to sleep. We were going around and shutting off lights, like we do every night, and I was in the front hall, and saw that a light was on upstairs. We were mostly living on the downstairs floor because of the dog's bad leg. We seldom went upstairs. By the way, Wally, even as a puppy, often used to sit at the bottom of those stairs just staring up at them. We didn't think anything of it at the time, because again we didn't believe in ghosts! We just thought he was a nutty puppy!

When I noticed that the light was on upstairs, I said, "Hey, Wendy, did you leave the light on upstairs?" And she replied that she hadn't been upstairs in about two weeks.

I said, "Neither have I. That's weird!"

So we decided to go upstairs to check it out. I armed myself with a broom, and Wendy with a Jaws paperback, and we looked around all of the upstairs and found nothing. Nothing was disturbed, the shutters were shut; everything was as it should be. We went into the blue room, and I thought maybe there was something there that we didn't know about. We were just trying to figure out a logical reason for the light.

We thought, "Well, somehow that just happened." We decided to just let it go, to forget about it and go to bed. We shut off the lights and got in bed.

We had just shut off the lights when we heard this BOOM! BOOM! BOOM! Really loud, three times! They were really very violent loud noises; so loud that we sat right up in bed.

Wendy said, "We are not going up there!"

"Oh, yes we are," I said. "We are not going to be like those victims in the movies. We are going to go up there and see what this is!"

So we grabbed the broom and the paperback and we headed back upstairs. We looked, and found... nothing. The shutters were fine, everything was normal.

We said, "Okay, that's weird, but what can we do? We just have to go back to bed and go to sleep." So we went to bed, and I just lay there. I watched the clock: midnight, one, two o'clock. It was between two and three, and I was in this weird kind of state, in and out of sleep, but sooo tired at the same time.

I looked at Wendy, and she was in this deep sleep, and I was thinking, "Gosh. I guess that really didn't bother her very much." But I was really freaked out, just lying there. Then I started hearing running upstairs. It kind of sounded like a fabric swishing across the floor, and I got so I couldn't even swallow. It was so freaky, and it sounded so otherworldly. It sounded like every bad horror movie; it was almost like someone was playing a joke on us. It was that ridiculous! It was like someone was running back and forth upstairs!

Then, I heard a little girl laughing! At this point, I didn't even want to hear it. I heard her yell, "Hey, Sue!"

And I was thinking, "Oh my God, oh my God!" I looked at Wendy, and I was thinking, "How can she sleep like that? Okay, I've gone crazy; it's all in my head! Was I really asleep, or it was the power of suggestion?" I thought, "Just let it go."

At that point it was four a.m., and the sun would be coming up at five. I finally got up, and I took the dog outside. When I came back in, Wendy was just getting up.

I said, "Well, that was a weird night."

She said, "Yeah."

I asked her, "Did you hear..."

"...a little girl?" She finished my sentence.

"Yes, you heard it?"

"Yes. I thought you were sleeping, and I didn't want to wake you up, because you would think I was crazy!"

"I thought you would think I was crazy!"

Then we thought, "Oh my God, we have to spend another night here!" We were wrecks. But we made it through the next night. We turned on a fan for white noise, and held pillows around our ears. We didn't want to hear it again, it scared us so. The next day we packed up and moved back to New York, with our new ghost stories.

Of course we called Fi, Wendy's mother, and told her, and she said, "Oh yeah, Joan stayed here in the blue room, and the door opened and shut, over and over, all night long!" And those are latched doors. We then looked up "ghosts" and "poltergeists," and learned that it was a common thing to notice smells, and also that bangs seem to come in threes, as a common number.

Wendy said she remembered waking up and hearing this girl's voice, and wondering at first, "Where is her mother?" The experience was like a very bad horror movie that sounded like it came from somewhere else, like an echo, as if from another dimension. It was as if someone used sound effects on the words. It was really bizarre!

When Jan said to me, "Did you hear...?" and I was able to complete her sentence, that just really did it for me! I was so scared I felt like I had cotton in my mouth; I couldn't breathe. I am a firm believer now. We have never had an experience quite like that again.

But we got this feeling, especially upstairs, and sometimes in another room downstairs, too. Even my niece, who one time was staying in the "bird room," said that while she was sleeping she felt like someone was watching her. It's just a really weird sensation.

We found out that some members of the Wing family used to live here, and so we wondered if they had a little girl that died in the house. We went over to the Wing Ring Cemetery one time, and we looked around and we found the grave of a six-year-old girl named Hannah. We wondered if she died here in this house. Who knows who it could be?

I mentioned at this point that it occurred to me when they first started talking about hearing a little girl's voice, that there used to be a schoolhouse two lots over, where the Cary Memorial Library is now, and that perhaps this ghost might be a ghost child who loved it here because of the school. I have been learning a lot from the psychics, Annette and Paula, and I related to Wendy and Jan that a ghost was a person who died and is stuck in time, and that often a ghost will haunt the area of a place where they felt safe or loved when they were alive.

Jan continued: Another thing that happened recently was that I was jogging last summer up Morrison Heights Road. I was just jogging along, and though usually I wear a headset, I was just jogging with no music. I could hear marching behind me. Not like one set of footsteps, but maybe ten people behind me marching. I stopped and turned around, and there was no one there at all. I thought to myself, "That is absolutely bizarre." So I continued jogging, maybe a half a mile, and I heard it again.

I came home and was a little freaked out about it, but I didn't say anything to anyone. But I decided to tell Wendy that I could hear marching behind me when I was jogging, for no logical reason.

Another time, Linda, our neighbor across the street, came over to visit, shortly after Patrick, another neighbor across the street, had died. She said that Patrick had said that there were Revolutionary soldiers in the area. Patrick had told her that he had been up on Morrison Heights Road, and he had said, "You could hear them marching up there." So she told me this story, when I had never told her my story!

I said, "Up Morrison Heights Road? I also heard them marching up Morrison Heights Road!"

I suggested that maybe Jan was sensitive to the spirit world when she told me that story. Wendy reminded her about the sea captain ghost that Jan had seen at her house at Ocean Point, when she was a child. Jan said that this ghost would do things like mess up the laundry after you'd folded it. It was as if he was a mischievous ghost, she said. She always thought it was someone playing tricks on her, because she had never really believed in ghosts before now.

Wendy and Jan said that since living here over this past winter, though they haven't experienced anything huge like that unbelievable night years ago, they still sometimes have unexplained events.

Jan continued: Right after Wendy's parents left last fall, we did have something strange happen. We don't use fabric sheets, but Wendy's mother had left a box on the dryer. We are anti-chemical. Suddenly there were about five fabric sheets in with the laundry. I thought, "That's weird," but maybe it was her mom's leftovers. So I searched inside the dryer and the washing machine to make sure there weren't any extra ones stuck in there. Sure enough, about four or five washes later, we found about ten fabric sheets in the laundry! So you know things like that happen. And sometimes we still hear noises in the night.

Wendy said, "We have so many nutty friends out in California, and we were always the naysayers! We are firm believers now, after staying in this house! Though we don't understand it, we just know that it is a mystery."

*Chapter 3*

# Greentrees in Mount Vernon

*This old house was easily one of the most haunted houses I encountered. The house itself was just amazing; it had the most antique-looking kitchen I have ever seen. Little work has been done over the years to change the house. It has been kept very true to the way it was when it was built, and had a very "old days" feel to it. My friend came with me on this visit, and the following is an account of our visit.*

David Caldwell, owner of the home at the time of our visit, and his ex-wife Rhonda, welcomed us to hear their ghost stories. This is where I was first introduced to medium clairvoyants Annette and Paula. We sat around the kitchen table, and they told us the following ghost stories. It was a wonderfully spooky afternoon.

David began by giving us some history about the house and his grandparents who lived there. David told us that his grandparents Helen Cushman and Erskine Caldwell lived in this very old and grand home called Greentrees.

David said Erskine was a famous writer who wrote the once

popular *Tobacco Road*. Erskine always said that he did his best work while living at Greentrees. David told us a story about Erskine, who was called a "Georgia Boy," and who had lived a prominent and sheltered life. Erskine's father was a preacher, and not an outdoorsman by any stretch. "The story goes that Erskine started cutting poplar trees in October. Some family members said, 'Oh yeah, that will burn like snowballs!' Yeah, my father said growing up in this house was… well, you would run all the way from your bedroom down to the kitchen to get warm in the mornings!" Helen was one of Erskine's five wives. When *Tobacco Road* hit Broadway, Erskine left Helen.

Helen Cushman was known around this area as the "Green Witch." She was famous for telling ghost stories, and throwing lavish Halloween parties. She was a wonderful storyteller, and there is quite a collection of stories that she used to write and tell. In fact, she used to be a creative decorator, and even once had a coffee table that looked like a coffin! Greentrees was well-known locally as a very haunted house for many years.

David said that his earliest memories of Helen were that she was always telling ghost stories and spinning yarns:

She would put my cousins and myself in the stories, and so forth. I came here for Christmas, summers, and vacations as a child, and I remember being alone upstairs, and feeling the hair stand up on the back of my neck. Then I would bolt for the stairs!

As a child, I don't think I necessarily had a definite sense of a spirit or ghost around, but the idea was never far from my mind. It was an immense house, and just scary on its own. I was always sort of respectful of it, (he laughs).

Helen had three children, one of whom was my father. I will tell one story that Helen used to tell. She used to have big parties, and there was a boy named David Kirk, who was the son of a best friend of hers from New York who was staying here, and the boy was upstairs sleeping in a crib. He was about two, or a little older at the time. He was sleeping in a high crib that did not have a side that went up and down. Helen said it was virtually impossible for him to have gotten out of the crib on his own. People were down here at the party socializing and drinking, and so forth. Well, he came down the stairs and was standing on the landing, and everyone was astonished, and asked him how he got out of his crib.

He said, "This woman just walked through the wall and picked me up and set me down, and I just thought I would come downstairs and tell you about it!" Later, this boy's parents both died tragically, and my grandparents adopted him, and he grew up living here with them.

Another story is that my father said he was practicing his violin one time upstairs, and his instructor used to have him sit in front of a mirror when he practiced, as it would help him somehow. Well, he said he looked up, and saw a ghost standing in the mirror behind him and his instructor! He was a pretty sober fellow, so it was amazing that he would even tell me a story like this.

Rhonda began by telling us, "A lot of things began happening when we started some renovations, and started tearing up some walls. At first, we thought that Helen was letting us know that she was around, because she always said that she would come back to visit after she died. An example is when we would be sitting down to eat, and we would smell something burning when we were halfway through our dinner. I would look at the stove, and every single one of the burners would be turned on! Lights would go on and off, things like that."

David said, "There was the time that a friend of Rhonda's came here and saw a ghost wearing a Civil War uniform, upstairs in the pool room. Now, I have heard this house was a stagecoach stop back in the 1860s and '70s, and people used to stay overnight here. I understand that the stagecoach ran from the coast up the river in Hallowell, through Fayette, and then up to Rangeley. Anyway, this friend, who had some psychic ability, felt that there were many spirits who couldn't move on, but were connected to this period in time."

Rhonda explained that a friend of theirs had come here because they were having such a problem with scary things happening in the house, and that David's children were pretty spooked at the time. This friend had instructed them to burn sage to get rid of the negative energy.

When we would have the kids on weekends or vacations, we started noticing that they wouldn't go upstairs by themselves. They would hold hands and then go upstairs, and it was just sort of an unspoken thing that they did. For example, the TV would go off and on by itself. The kids reported that they were hearing noises, and they compared it to playing a record on warp speed, and it would just go really, really fast. I remember some of the cousins were seeing little flashing lights in the bedroom.

When we started doing renovations, we heard footsteps, and there were doors opening in parts of the house that we weren't using. It was wintertime, and there were parts of the house that we were not heating of course, and we would find those doors open.

I was telling a man that I work with stories about things that were happening here. He said, "I can come over and help you help them (the spirits) to move on." So we just started burning sage, and walking through the house, and he said that some spirits will go and some won't, but that he didn't sense any bad spirits here. The house did sort of have a different feel to it after that. It didn't seem, I don't know, as oppressed. But, for example, David's daughter got up one time in the middle of the night and saw a ghost outside in the bathroom hallway. I remember that she had been sick, and had slept late, and when she came downstairs in the morning, she didn't look well.

I said, "Caitlyn, what's the matter?"

"Well, you're not going to believe this, but I saw something last night."

"What did you see?"

She said, "I got up to go to the bathroom in the night, and there was this woman standing next to the door. She had on this red dress and her hair was pulled back into a bun, and she had on boots that had buttons going up the side."

It was a short time after that, when we were going through some things in the attic that we found this photo of the woman that she had described, to a "T"!

David added that there was a framed needlepoint piece which read, "As we mourn our loss."

"We think she may have died in the house, and that she is still here."

Rhonda remembered that David's son, Sam, when he was about two or three, came down the stairs one time, after having gone to bed.

I said, "What's the matter, Sam, how come you're not asleep?"

He said, "That man scares me." Now, we didn't know who he was referring to, but he was too young to really verbalize what he had seen.

I remember when our daughter woke up one night, repeatedly, and I said, "Why don't you just come and get into bed with us?" It was one of those nights that was pitch black outside, and you couldn't see your hand in front of your face.

So we got her into bed with us, and after a few minutes she just sat right up in bed and said, "Who is that?"

I said, "There is no one here but your dad and me." She kept insisting, and I said "Honey, there is no one here!"

She kept insisting, so I asked, "Well, where is he?"

She sat straight up in bed and said, "He's right there!" as she pointed right at the foot of the bed.

Rhonda acknowledged that she had felt spooked a lot when she was alone in the house, and told me the following story:

Quite often when David was in Massachusetts, I would sit here and have every light on in the house, and the TV and the radio, on too. I would sit here during the week, when David was gone and the kids weren't here yet, and I would be so scared! But it got worse when we started doing renovations. I remember one time when David had been taking classes at Farmington, and on this particular day he was home sick in bed. It was during the day, and I had the day off from work. I was sitting right here. I was reading the newspaper, and it was very quiet. I didn't have the radio on or anything, and David was upstairs sleeping. I heard footsteps, and they were very, very light. It was like a small woman, or a child, and it was like they were trying to be very quiet.

I would hear two to three footsteps; then they would stop. I thought, "Did I just hear something?" And I would go back to reading the newspaper. Then I heard it again. I thought, "Oh my gosh," and I went to the foot of the stairs, and the hair on the back of my neck went straight up! It was obvious that it was in the hallway straight up at the top of the stairs! And I was thinking, "Oh my gosh," because it is such a big house, and it was just me and him here. I was thinking, "Is someone living here in this house without our knowing it? Are they in another ell, or is somebody hiding out in this house?" So I went running up the stairs, making as much noise as I could, hoping that would scare them away. Well, of course, there was nothing there. I opened up the bedroom door, and David was just snoring away.

I woke him up and said, "David did you just get up and use the bathroom or something?"

Of course he said, "No, you're losing it!' And he didn't believe me at the time.

There were many other strange things that happened. Sometimes, I would go outside to hang up clothes on the clothesline, and I would come back to the door and it would be locked. I would think, okay it's not funny anymore, and of course, I wouldn't have a key.

Sometimes when David would be away all week, I would go stay with my mother in Farmington, and we would ride up there together.

I remember one time we came home, had dinner, and watched a little TV. Then we went up to go to bed, and I went into the bathroom. There is a door up there that goes into the other part of the house, and that door was wide open. We never used that door, especially in the wintertime, and it was always closed. I asked David about it, but he said that he did not open the door. So we headed to bed. In the hallway there is another room down from our bedroom. There is a door on that room that is painted shut, and that door was open!

I said to David, "Now do you believe me?" I don't think either one of us slept very well that night. The next morning we both woke up before the alarm clock went off. We were just lying there talking, when all of a sudden we heard someone running outside in the hallway! Well, David flew out of bed and ran down that hallway, and there was nothing there. Nothing.

I was here last summer visiting, and David's family was here, and we were all outside. I don't know why, but I came into the house, for a drink or something. I heard footsteps again.

David's sister had a strange experience here, too. I don't know if she'd want her name used or not but, one time when she was in college, she came here to visit her grandmother for the weekend. She was in bed reading, and she lay back on her pillow and rubbed her eyes. She looked up at the ceiling, and she said she could see women appear, and they were holding hands, dancing in a circle above her! She said she wasn't scared, but she said she had a feeling that they wanted her to come with them, and she just said no.

David told us that David Kirk had looked into the history of some of the families who had lived in the house early on. "Helen's father had bought this house in 1902. We also discovered that the house was built by a wealthy Virginian who had fought in the Revolutionary War with George Washington, had come up here after the war, and was a timber chaser. He built a lot of the small mills in this area, using waterfalls for power. He was credited with naming this town Mount Vernon, because he thought it was very much like Mount Vernon, Virginia where Washington lived. His name was Noah Greeley. There were some other families that lived here too, throughout the 1800s, until my great-grandfather bought it."

Annette, who had been carefully listening to the stories, finally spoke.

I am a medium clairvoyant, she said, and this is what I do. I go to houses and check them out and see if there are any ghosts or spirits, because I can see and talk to them. Paula can, as well. Rhonda had mentioned this house to me, and said that it has been haunted for years and years. So I said I would love to see it, because this is what I love to do!

Paula and I came to this house, and we saw both ghosts and spirits in the house. We walked into the kitchen first, and we didn't really see anything there, but when we walked into the library, or living room, as it is called now, I sensed that it used to be a dining room years ago. Now, my spirit guides help me when I walk into a house because sometimes the ghosts and spirits don't want to talk. Sometimes they are just very polite, and are very respectful, too. Anyway, in that room

I saw a man coming down the stairs wearing a suit coat.

Actually, he is here right now. I can see him, and I don't know if he's trying to be very polite, or if he's minding his own business, but he has his back to us. He is a very big-shouldered man, but I would not say that he is an overweight man, and he's just standing there. He is doing the same thing as when I saw him that first time I was here. When I first saw him coming down the stairs, I couldn't see above his shoulders; I couldn't see his head because of the ceiling from the upstairs as he came down, because he was so tall. I couldn't see his face, and he still won't show me his face. I don't know who this man is, but he is apparently one of your ghosts in this house. It's almost like he is conducting business, and of course being a ghost, he is living in his own time, in his own world.

David said that the description of this man sounded like his grandfather.

Annette continued to tell us about her first time here:

Next we went into another living room, or study, perhaps, where there was a Victorian couch, and that room was filled with spirits and ghosts. Now again, ghosts are living in their own time and they are not always aware of us, and they haven't crossed over yet. Spirits, of course, are the souls who have crossed over and are here to visit. They know they are dead. I told Rhonda and the people who were here at the time that this room was filled with spirits and ghosts, and the spirits were acting like they were celebrating and socializing in this room!

My friend Paula had just come out of one of the bedrooms and said she had seen a lady ghost in there. I sent her back in, told her to go back in and talk to her, and she did.

We went on, and were walking up by the bathroom, and Rhonda was relating her story about the ghost lady that her daughter saw. We didn't see anything right there, but as we went past this cloak room in the hallway, a Civil War man appeared.

Now, before I even came here, I had this feeling that there was a grave marker up the hill from the house, and that it belonged to a Civil War person. I had asked Rhonda about this. She knew of the grave marker as I described it near the house.

Well, this ghost saw us coming through the hall, and he said "Oh, lady friends!"

I started chuckling, and I said, "Who are you?"

He said he was from the Civil War, and that when he was alive, people would come here for weeks at a time in the summer, for training. But he added that at night, there was entertainment and dancing in what he called the Great Hall. He said that it was a very pretty place at night, all lit up with lanterns. He told me that the women would come by in the evenings, by stagecoach. He said they would be dropped off here, and that a lot of the soldiers were single men. He was telling me that there were paths that they walked on at night, and they were lit by lanterns as well, and that it was very romantic. He said that they would go on the paths to a lake. I asked Rhonda if there was a lake or pond down that way, and she said yes, so that validated what I heard.

The ghost said to me, "Today I didn't go, I stayed home because I was sick. My men are out practicing." He actually seemed to be aware of us, and to know that he was a ghost. I usually try to cross ghosts over when I see them, but this one, for some reason, I did not.

Another experience I had the first time I came here was that we came into this room and I heard someone go, "Shhh!" I didn't know what it was about, until we walked into the next room and Paula said she saw a little boy who appeared to be playing hide and seek. We guessed that these ghost children were playing hide and seek and saying, "Shhh!" to us as we came into the room! Basically, those are all the stories I have about the first time I was here in this house, and I am interested in seeing what we will find today.

Paula, who prefers to be described as an "intuitive," also spoke about her recent impressions at Greentrees:

Now, the first time I came here with Annette, we actually did a drive-by! As we drove by, I looked up in the window, and I saw this blond-haired girl looking out the upstairs window at us. I wasn't sure at first if I was seeing things.

So, on the first visit I saw another ghost, a young boy, about age seventeen, and he was sitting on a windowsill. When I first saw the blond-haired girl up in the window that day, she was turning her head as if she was responding to someone beside her. I saw the same young boy, who was dressed in dark pants and shirt and jacket. Then I saw the girl again. It was as if she was hiding, and I realized that they were playing hide and seek!

On our first visit here, I also saw a man wearing a brown suit, sitting in the library. I don't always see the same things that Annette does. When we had gone upstairs, as we went through the bedrooms, I saw this woman. She was a little on the heavy side, and she was bending over and picking something up.

She said, "I am so tired of picking up after them all the time!" So I went into the room where Rhonda and Annette and Rhonda's daughter Molly were, and I told them what I saw. Annette asked me to go right back in there and talk to her.

Well, I felt kind of odd, because seeing ghosts and spirits is new to me! The ghost spoke in broken English, and I was getting some kind of accent, and her name was Marguerite. I got the impression from her that she was a maid. I asked her what she did for work, and she said she was in charge of a lot of people. She said she was tired of picking up after everybody.

As we went back to the main house, I was the last one coming through the door, and I heard this same woman saying, "Go, go, go!"

I said to her, "We are not here to make more work for you."

Annette asked if she was ever married, and I heard her say, "No I never had time for that!" I realized that she was listening and responding to what we were saying! It was weird.

Then Rhonda asked, "Should we cross her over?"

All of a sudden, as Annette was saying, "You might feel like you are being pulled," I was thinking, "Oh my gosh."—that's exactly what was happening! It was really like she was being sucked back from the way that she came! And then she was gone.

Annette added that as she was hearing Paula talking about this woman, she became aware of this woman ghost. All Annette could think was, "Oh my gosh, this woman has been cleaning this house for an eternity!"

"Yeah, we need to let her go. Help her cross over!"

Paula told us that when she was in the living room, she happened to look up, and the woman was at the top of the stairway looking down at her, and said "Thank you!" and then she was gone!

Paula continued to talk about their first visit there. She said they had all walked into a room out over the barn, and she felt very dizzy and sick when she stepped into the room. Annette thought that Paula was reacting to the feelings of a ghost.

David had earlier told one of Helen's stories about a man who reportedly used to drink too much, and he had a peg leg. He had lived in the attic space, and there was also a cook who worked in the kitchen who was mischievous. In this story, which David said was one hundred fifty years old, the cook had unscrewed this man's prosthetic leg, and had caused the man to fall down the stairs, and he broke his neck.

Annette wondered if this story related to Paula's feelings when she stepped into the barn. Annette explained that sometimes a medium clairvoyant can pick up on the way a person felt on the last day that he or she was alive, and that it was possible Paula was picking up on the feelings of the ghost that had been drunk and dizzy.

"Sometimes a ghost will communicate their feelings to a person who is sensitive," Annette said. "Sometimes it's the only way they have to explain how they were feeling, and to tell their story. It's like they are saying, 'This is how I died, or this is how I was feeling.' That is my understanding anyway, so that is what I try to teach people. I believe the way Paula was feeling was the result of a ghost trying to communicate their own feelings to her. For some reason, I feel like Paula's feeling were connected to that story about the man with the prosthetic, and I believe he did drink too much, and I think that's exactly what happened to him. He was drunk and fell down the stairs."

Later, as we walked into the large living room, Annette told us that she heard someone say, "Beautiful, beautiful memories here."

She said, "She is definitely an 1800s era ghost, and she is wearing a big puffy pink dress that goes all the way down to the floor. She said, 'I have a bonnet.' She is speaking to me now, saying 'Yes, I am a ghost.'

"She is with other women who are walking around. She says this is a very beautiful, beautiful place. So yes, right now there is a ghost here from the Victorian age, it seems. And yes, there are other women here, too, and there are also two men, one of which is the man that Paula sees, who is wearing a brown suit."

As we explored the house and all of the rooms, Annette and Paula pointed out where they had seen the spirits and ghosts on the first visit. They continued to describe the ghosts and spirits as they saw them on this visit, too. Greentrees is certainly an awesome old house that was used for many years to entertain, and to shelter many travelers and soldiers in the years past. The ghosts and spirits were people who loved it so much that they apparently didn't want to leave. I could relate to that feeling. Though it needed a lot of work, the house was just amazing.

Annette, a short time after our visit, told me this account of her follow-up visit there:

Paula and I went back to Greentrees because David had called us and told us that since our last visit, the house had become very active again. David had called Paula and stated, "I think we made the house angry, because it has become noisier than ever!"

I told Paula to tell David that the last time we were there we crossed over the lady in the beautiful gown. Perhaps because we never took the time to cross the others over, they know that the lady is gone, and they can feel the absence of her energy. I felt after we left that they were trying to get somebody's attention.

David said, "You need to come quickly!" because he was so concerned.

So Paula and I drove down, and this time I could see the man in the brown suit that Paula had seen before—the one with a martini and cigar. David asked us if we could actually see them and talk to them, and I said yes. I said, "We need to cross them over, and that is why they are so loud."

David said, "Before you do, I want to talk to my grandfather."

So I said, "Go ahead."

David began this beautiful speech. I can't remember what he said exactly, but it was from his heart. David had heard so many wonderful things about his grandfather being a pillar of society and so on, and so he told his grandfather how much he admired him, and that he just loved the fact that he was his grandfather.

As he was saying this, I said, "Your grandfather is right here and he is listening to you."

He said, "Really?"

I said, "Yes," and so he went on.

He said the rest of what he wanted to say to his grandfather, and he got teary-eyed. In the end, I said, "It is time for your grandfather to cross over, but first he wants to say something to you."

So the grandfather said to the grandson, "Thank you for taking such good care of the house. Thank you. It is okay to let it go. You have my blessing." This was such a relief for David, who was very attached emotionally to the house, but was seriously considering selling it, because it was too large to take care of and to heat. The grandfather had given him permission to sell the house. Then I saw the grandfather crossing over.

Then I saw the man in the brown suit, and I told him it was time to cross over, and he said, "Yes, I understand, but let me say my goodbyes first."

He went in the other room to find the lady ghost on the couch. I guess he was really attached to this house, because Paula had seen him previously sitting on the couch. He had said, "Come here; let me talk to you," to someone at that time. I think that room meant a lot to him, so that's where he went before he crossed over.

David suggested that I go upstairs to the Great Room to look for the Civil War ghost. I saw the Civil War ghost coming down those beautiful stairs with the wooden banister. There was no one around, just me, and I looked up at him and I smiled, and then I put my hands together and I said to him, "You are going on a journey!"

And he said, "Yes, I know!"

I said, "Yes, you are going to cross over and go to where your loved ones are; your wife and your children."

He said, "I understand, and I want to thank you, Annette." He said my name, and I was shocked; that really startled me!

So I said, "I wish you a wonderful journey, and goodbye!"

He was all smiles, and I was smiling, and I blew him a kiss, because I really liked him. And then he was gone.

The whole house just felt lifted, and I went into the kitchen, and I turned to David and I said, "All clean. All gone. There is nothing here."

"Are you sure?"

I said, "I'm positive. There are no more ghosts."

There are spirits now; we all come with spirits around us and with our spirit guides. There will be spirits here as long as there are people here. But as far as ghosts or any haunting, the house is all clean, and it will be nice for the new owners who buy this house. I said to him that the house already feels light to me, and I told him that he would notice that, too. I told him that every now and then someone may hear something, but that will be their own spirit guides around them.

*Chapter 4*

# A Recollection by Hannah Faulkner

Early in the 1960s when I was living and working in New York City, my sister Martha was a student at Kents Hill School. Visiting my family in Maine over the Christmas holidays, I heard some unusual tales related by Martha. She gave me an excited, breathless account of her recent evening at Greentrees hosted by David Kirk for school friends.

Martha said that David had told the group about an evening when he was a young child. His parents had put him to bed in his secure crib upstairs in Greentrees so that he would sleep while they entertained guests below. Later, the guests were surprised when David unexpectedly appeared among them. When his parents asked how he had gotten out of his crib, he said that "a nice lady" had lifted him out so that he could come downstairs and join the party. No one among the guests had been upstairs.

At David's party, Martha sat on a sofa chatting with other guests. When she happened to look out the window, she saw the face of a man wearing a trench coat pass by towards the door. "Oh, David," she said, "someone else is coming to our party."

"How do you know that?"

Martha said, "I just saw a man pass by the window."

"No one could walk past that window, because it is one story above the ground. You must have seen a ghost."

Hearing Martha's tales that winter gave me chills, which I still experience today thinking about the events.

*Chapter 5*

# FULL MOON OF JULY
## by Helen Cushman Caldwell

*This story was told by Helen many years ago, and is printed here with permission of her grandson, David Caldwell.*

Far more than witches or ghosts or things that go bump in the night, as children we feared the evil that lurked abroad on the night of the full moon of July on Thirty Mile River. As much as we might scoff at superstition, or flaunt our courage by walking slowly by the graveyards near the northwest branch, we did not venture on the lake on the night of the full moon of July. If, on a dare, some of us did paddle up the lake on such a night, we did not go again, nor did we ever speak of the terror that lay waiting beneath the waters.

On any other night in the year, we would paddle blithely for miles, even in the dark of the moon, directing our canoes by the stars or the outline of Vienna Mountain or the Headland or Laird's Ledge. But on that night of nights, we would eschew the lake as if by a strange unspoken agreement. We never knew exactly what we feared or why,

33

we simply did not discuss it. Had my wise father known of this taboo, I'm sure he would have routed us out from beside the fireplace, and made us paddle the lake from one end to the other until dawn broke. For to him, a fear must be brought out in the open and examined.

Years passed, and we grew up and married and had children and grandchildren of our own. The full moon of July was no more important than any other full moon, certainly not one when we would avoid the lake. We had long ago forgotten the taboo, or buried it in these dim recesses of our minds where we hide our other childish fears.

Suddenly, a few weeks ago, the door to that closed recess swung open. We were invited far up the lake to a party. Come, the invitation read, On the Night of The Full Moon of July. Involuntarily, I shuddered at the prospect, and then I remembered the old taboo. Questions crowded my mind. Why had this been a date to strike terror in us when we were young? Was there ever any real basis for our dread? Searching for an answer, I began the long journey back to the days of my youth.

Then, as clearly as if it had happened last year, I recalled a night in July over fifty years ago. There were many of us in three canoes and two Rangeley boats leaving before the full moon rose to go up the lake to the Headland for a picnic in the moonlight. With us was a beloved old Indian who knew the waters far better than most white men. It was very still on the water. Any spoken word traveled back to the craft behind us. And the Indian, who was paddling in the stern of the lead canoe, said, "Never go up this lake through the west channel on the night of the full moon of July. The moon, which controls the waters of the earth, also rules over the monsters which lie deep beneath the surf. During this month of that moon of July, the dreadful creatures come up from their caves to see the moon. Nbesit the night walker and the evil Kurowesak who dwells in the cliffs above the west channel come down and jump in the craft of the unwise ones who dare venture into their bath. Many a brave has drowned when his canoe sank from the unseen weight; sank into the waiting claws of the monster below. And their allies, the evil dwarves above, marked up another tally on the rock ledges."

With that, the Indian swerved the lead canoe to the right, and four of the craft passed the channel to the rocks off the Headland. Behind us, one canoe filled with "old people"—in this case, college students—turned unheedingly to the left and into the west channel.

I remember so well the scornful laughter of the boys as they shouted in derision and waved goodbye to us. At that moment, a strange and ominous cloud obscured the full moon of July, a mist rose from the waters, and we could not see ten feet ahead. The old Indian stopped paddling, went ashore and built a fire, and shook his head, muttering to himself in Abenaki. After an interminable time, it seemed, the mist rose, and we continued on our journey.

On the picnic rocks, the Indian built a fire, and we waited and waited, but the third canoe did not appear. As hungry as we always were, we had little appetite that night. It was after midnight when the Indian put out the fire and we started back down the lake. I'm sure one of us looked into the west channel as we paddled to the north of Birch Island.

Silently and rapidly we paddled, to get off the water before those monsters could leave the west channel and find us. Not until the moon had set did the arrogant boys return—white, trembling, and obviously shaken. They refused to say what had happened, and left in a day or so for the south. But their canoe was marked with huge scratches, gouged out with sharp claws. None of us ever rode in that canoe again.

Only this week, in an old book of Indian legends I read of a similar superstition among the nomadic branch of the powerful Anasagunticooks, the Caghnaugas, who dwelt along Thirty Mile River. Translated and revised, it was something like this: When the moon and the sun and earth are in a straight line (i.e., in syzygy) in the time of the hot moon, avoid the waters where evil waits for those who pass by. Even the strongest brave will faint or be carried underneath to be held captive in the lair of the serpents…on this night of the full moon of July.

*Chapter 6*

# Stevenson's Brick Farmhouse

Annette and I visited the home of Betty and Craig Stevenson in Wayne. Annette told us that before she left her home that day, her spirit guides were suggesting she wear something Native American. As she drove by Betty's house in her car, she was "told" to keep driving past the house and to stop at the Beech Hill Cemetery. Annette said she was getting Native American vibes around this area. As she approached the Beech Hill Cemetery, her spirit guides asked her to stop. She looked up and saw the name "Hood." Annette felt that the name "Hood" was somehow connected to the Stevenson's place.

"Right now, I feel this place is filled with many ghosts and spirits," she said. She felt that Betty's home had something to do with "Holy ground," though she wasn't sure why.

Betty said, "Ever since we worked on the house and opened up the kitchen, there is just something about it. It is a very different house, and it just loves to be filled up with people; you can just feel it." Betty said that she gets a feeling around the area of the kitchen door, and that it just keeps opening.

"On a Sunday when I'm in there cooking, that door just opens all the time. It just gets to the point where I look up and say, 'Oh, hi!' I think of the presence as my cooking buddy. The aroma of the kitchen just seems to call him in; he spends a lot of time here."

Annette said, "I see the ghost of a woman who is bent over, and who is very small. She is carrying a tray. I'm getting that she is Native American or somehow related to Native Americans. She looked like she worked very, very hard, and I'm not sure if she actually lived here or not. I feel like she's going right through me, and she seems very happy that we are here. She was very old, but she was not from this farm. I think she was a servant from somewhere nearby. She said she thought she would just come by today to say hello. She likes to come visit you when you are cooking. Yes, she looks like she worked very hard, and she is a petite little thing. She says she is not the spirit that you are talking about, Betty, but she likes to come visit you, too. She is a very dark-skinned woman, and yes, I would say she is maybe Native American, maybe Chippewa."

Then the ghost confirmed to Annette that her parents were from "away."

Annette continued, "She does look very sad, though, like she is doing her duty, but she is working very hard, and I am saying that she looks sad, yet she says she is happy to be here. I would say that she is a ghost, not a spirit. Again, she comes to visit you, but she is not from here. In fact, she is pointing that way."

Betty said that the Norlands church steeple, in Livermore Falls, could be seen from her kitchen window looking out in that direction. It is possible that this ghost was a servant from the Norlands Plantation. We all looked to the west, and admired the view of the mountains, where the steeple of the church was visible in the distance. Annette suggested that the ghost woman probably liked Betty's energy, and visited her often.

Grace, one of Betty's Reiki sisters, who was also present during our visit, told us she could see a small female ghost as well. Grace explained that she often saw the woman standing by the door of the kitchen, though she didn't know why. Grace said she had a sense that the woman had lived in this farmhouse before, and that the woman had "gatherings," and so she thought that was why she was always by the door.

Annette said she thought that the woman did not live here, she was a servant, and perhaps she waited by the door because it was her job to welcome people through the door. Annette said the woman told her that this was a working farm, not a fancy farm. Annette thought that the Native American woman that she was seeing was different from the woman that Grace was seeing.

Grace told us she had also sensed the male spirit that Annette had seen, but that the male had a stronger presence. Betty said she felt that the male spirit or ghost was a very friendly presence, and always had a smile. Annette felt that this male was an uncle of Betty's. Betty did not know who this might be. Annette described the male as wearing a Bordeaux hat, perhaps to help Betty later identify who he was, if she, for example, came across a picture of a great uncle or someone else, in the future.

As we walked into the big open, rustic dining room beside the kitchen, Betty said, "This room is a funny room that doesn't seem to hold a lot of people well. I can load this table up with food, and people will not come in here and eat very much. This room will not entertain a lot of people. I am not kidding you; people will not eat in here unless they are sitting down at the table. Really, people do not like to hang out in this room at all."

Betty talked about a special place out back on the property, which both she and her husband Craig, and her Reiki sisters call, "Fairyland."

"It's a place where I believe there are vibrations or impressions of the earliest settlers in this area, perhaps even the Pilgrims." Betty said that when you go to this particular place, "You just feel speechless, for as long as people will let you. It is sacred ground; there is no doubt about it." Betty said her husband Craig especially feels a deep connection to this place.

Annette stated, "In fact, this place is so special to him that it seemed to him like he had been in this place before, in a past life. He recognizes this as his home, though he may not even consciously realize that."

Betty's Reiki sisters also added that Fairyland makes one feel an innocence and light joy that is very magical.

"It's like literally being a child and going back in time when you are down there," said Grace.

Betty added, "I think the whole place, including the house, just feels like such a happy place that anyone can feel the joy; like a kid in a candy store!"

After touring the farmhouse, we re-entered the dining room. Annette said that the room was full of many spirits and ghosts. She felt that they liked being in this room, and that the spirits themselves liked to sit around the large table in the old chairs. Annette thought that the reason that Betty's guests did not want to sit down in these chairs or hang around in this room—and perhaps the reason the room had such a "full" feeling to it—was because of the many spirits and ghosts here.

This farmhouse definitely had a feeling of the past to it, and we all experienced a special vibe being there that afternoon.

*Author's note: Grace, a free spirit, passed away unexpectedly of an illness about a year after this interview. Betty tells me that she and her Reiki sisters always feel Grace's beautiful and strong presence in "Fairyland."*

*photograph courtesy of Mike Ketchen*

*Chapter 7*

# Dave's Appliance Store and the Ketchen House

*Dave's Appliance Store is located in one of the many buildings formerly serviced by the old railroad system on Western Avenue in Winthrop. Originally, it was Maxim's Feed and Grain store, from the early 1900s throughout the 1980s. The old building has many large sprawling rooms, now used to house the appliance business.*

Brothers Brian and Mike Ketchen shared their ghost stories with us. They own the family business together with their brother Scott. Their parents, Dave and Dee Ketchen, started the very successful appliance business. The family lived for many years in the house across the street from Dave's Appliance Store, where Mike now lives with his wife Miranda and their two children.

We explored both places, and both were haunted by many ghosts and spirits. Annette and her sister Diane, also a gifted psychic medium, agreed to visit, and to interpret the haunting. As we arrived at the store, Annette and Diane told me that they had both just seen ghosts looking out of the upstairs windows of Mike's house, and they described the ghosts as waving and smiling, anxious for us to come and visit. It's always interesting to hang out with psychics!

Betty (Jackson) Stevenson joined us for the visit, too, because she had grown up in the Ketchen house in the 1960s and 70s. She too experienced some of the same exact eerie occurrences at the house which were disturbing the Ketchens now.

Standing outside Dave's Appliance Store and looking over at

the house, Annette immediately picked up on a feeling of sadness, pinpointing it to the back stairway of the Ketchen house. Mike said that both his wife Miranda and brother Brian have always felt as if they were being chased by someone when they walked up that back stairway. Betty told us about a room that was accessed from the top of those stairs, which went out over the barn. The barn was torn down in the early 1970s. She said that she and her siblings would never go into the top of the barn.

"It's the same thing," she said, "with the back stairway exactly. We felt very scared there, and we also felt like we were being chased when we walked up the stairs. When I think back on it even now, it makes my heart pound."

Annette told us that she immediately got a very heavy feeling from the direction of where the old barn used to be. She asked if there had been a "hanging" there. Annette said that she definitely felt a male presence, left over from someone who may have had some mental health problems, or was suicidal before he died. She said she clearly saw a vision of a hangman's noose, but she wasn't seeing a body associated with it, and so she wasn't sure what this meant.

Betty spoke up and said the word "noose" had triggered a memory for her, and that she remembered seeing a noose in the barn hanging high up on a beam near a broken window when she was a child. She also remembered that she and her siblings instinctively believed that someone had died up there in that room.

Mike told us that when his parents had bought the house years ago, he played a lot in that room up over the barn. "We got away with that for about a week or two, and then Dad sealed the door off, and wouldn't allow us out there for some reason."

Annette again said she got a "very, very negative feeling" from a room located near the top of the back stairway.

Mike said that when his daughter was about two years old, this room was her baby room. "She had slept through the night every night since the day we brought her home; she was a mellow baby. Then there was something that spooked her in that bedroom one night, and she was hysterical. She would never go back into that room again."

Annette said that she was getting a male presence with a heavy and negative feeling associated with this part of the house. She asked about the attic, and where it was located. She was able to describe the attic space correctly to Mike and Betty, without having seen it. She told us that she was getting a negative feeling from the attic, as well as the room that used to be over the barn. Betty agreed that she also had a bad feeling about the attic, and in fact, she said she never went up there at all as a child.

"I used to play up there when I was a kid," Mike said. "It used to be our hangout; and some pretty weird things used to happen up there." He said that the attic space has new insulation there now and that it is basically a closed off space.

Annette and Diane both thought that this house and the appliance store were very active with spirits and ghosts because of the rich history, and all the people in the town who were associated with the railroad. Annette said, "Being a railroad town—as the spirits are referring to it—it was a very busy place. I have never been to this town before today, and the spirits are telling me it was an extremely busy place."

Mike asked if we wanted to go look out in the warehouse area of Dave's Appliance Store, and Annette laughed and said, "No, they (ghosts and spirits) are all in here!" She said that the spirits were fascinated with the modern appliances, and in fact, that they liked playing with the stoves. "Many of them are from the 19th century, so they are like, whoa, what is this?"

Brian had been ill and wasn't able to be present during our first visit there. Mike told us that Brian had always had bad dreams—almost on a nightly basis—about the house, which is also where they grew up. The dreams, he told us, were especially about the basement.

Betty spoke up and said, "As kids, we really believed that there was a man in the basement. You could hear him on the stairs. He only came out at night. I never went down in the cellar, never any further than the bottom stair. I was scared to death of the cellar. It used to be a dirt cellar when I was there. I still will not go down there because of how it made me feel. The man hung out over in the back corner against a wall made of stone. And he was always like this, crouched down."

"Could you see him?" Annette asked.

"We saw him, though we never saw his face. He was like this:

always hiding his face and crouched over. If I ever did go to the bottom step for some reason, I always felt like I was being chased back up the stairs."

Betty told us that her brother, had a terrible experience one summer when his father had him collect and stack all the old bricks down in the dirt cellar. She said that he was petrified the whole time. "My father was going to sell them," Betty explained.

The Jackson family bought this house in the early 1960s, and they sold it to Dave and Dee Ketchen around 1971.

When asked about how old the house was, Mike said that he had a picture of the house from the year 1900. He added that when he had been doing some work a couple of years before, he found some old coffee cans in the walls that had paper labels on them, and when he researched them he found that they were from the around 1870 or so. "I was hoping that they would be stuffed with money!" he joked. "Somebody must have stuck them in behind the old plaster that many years ago."

Mike told us about a ghost who appeared there often, and was witnessed by his employees at Dave's Appliance Store. He called the ghost, "the hand lady." His workers blamed "the hand lady" for every little noise or anything unusual that happened.

Betty told us that this story triggered another memory for her: there was a game that she and her siblings had played when they were little, called the "golden arm game." She wondered if, looking back, there was a reason that they played that game, and perhaps it was not random.

As we walked over to the house across the street, Annette explained that she got that the ghost in the cellar was not being negative, but rather that he had been hiding from the Jackson children years ago, so as not to scare them.

Annette believed the negativity came from the man in the barn, who may have been suicidal. "He doesn't want to cross over; he is stubborn." Annette explained to us. "He is wearing a dark coat, almost like a raincoat. Perhaps my spirit guides are only showing me this because you asked me what he looked like, but otherwise I wasn't seeing a descriptive vision of him. He is tall, and medium built. It is dark, and they are not showing me very much of him, and only from the back."

Annette's sister Diane could also see both ghosts; the negative man from over the barn, and the man who was crouching and hiding in the cellar. Diane described the crouching man as being in a submissive position, as if shying away from people.

Back upstairs in the house, Annette could also sense Mike's grandmother's spirit in the room near the hearth and the rocking chair. Mike shared that his grandmother did pass away peacefully, right there in that room. Annette gave the message from the grandmother to Mike that she loved the house, and the renovations they had made. This grandmother had lived in the house with Mike and his parents when he was growing up.

Annette and Diane felt that this was a very busy and active house spiritually. Annette was able to banish the negative man from the house with help from her spirit guides. She said that he was like a "grouchy" ghost, who was being very stubborn, but would never have caused any harm to anyone in the house. Annette added that she was getting more information about this ghost, and that he had died around the era of the 1920s or '30s, and that he was, as all ghosts are, just stuck in that time. Annette said she wanted to keep him separate from the other ghosts and spirits in the house, so that she could focus on the others.

Miranda told us that the top of the stairway on the other side of the house was the location where Brian had always dreamed about the door opening, and he said there would be old couple standing there at the top. She said that he dreamed of this almost every night, and that it was one of the few stories he was willing to share. She added that there were many other things he said happened to him that he did not want to talk about.

While we were upstairs, Betty told us about an incident where her parent's bedroom door kept coming open, and they would be constantly blaming it on the kids. Annette said it was because this particular bedroom wasn't meant to be a bedroom, and so the spirits and ghosts wanted to keep it open. The room was originally intended to be open, because it was a formal sitting room. Annette felt that the outside door, which was at the bottom of this stairway, was originally the formal front door of the house, and that guests would come into the house, and go up the steps and enter into this particular room for visits. Annette's vision was that this happened in the horse-and-buggy days.

"They would whoosh the guests up here into the parlor." She said the guests would refresh themselves, because they were dusty and tired, while the owners would prepare food for them downstairs. Annette said that a female spirit, who was telling her about these things, was the same spirit who told her that the door needed to be kept open for the guests.

Miranda said that she and her son Mitchell have actually heard the doorknob turn and the door open, even as recently as the night before.

Mike said Mitchell would nervously look at his mother and say, "Mom….!?" when it would happen, as if hoping for an explanation.

As we walked through the adjoining rooms upstairs which went across to the other side of the house where the spooky room was (on the barn side of the house), Betty, who had not been in this house since she was very young, said she felt she was literally walking down memory lane. We walked through the hallway to where the door was back when the barn was still attached to the house. We stood in the doorway of the room at the end of this hall where Michaela's bedroom was when she was a baby. Betty remembered that her father used to keep head mountings of animals like mountain sheep in that room. "It was always empty," she said, "always, except for those things that he kept in there."

Mike said that his parents had made this part of the house into an apartment, and that this had been his grandmother's room. Now, he said, it's where the family's six pug dogs sleep together, and while they do once in a while get spooked in this room, he added, "Usually, they go to bed, and they kennel up in there and they are fine; but once in a while they just go crazy!"

Annette felt that the source of all the haunting in this room was indeed the negative man. She added that now that the negative man was banished from the house, she was getting no more bad feelings, and so this room was now "clean."

At the top of the infamous stairs, Annette said she was getting the name "Tom." Miranda said that whenever she felt like she was being chased up these stairs, once she got to the top landing, she felt she was safe, like he couldn't go past that point.

Annette suggested that it would be therapeutic for Betty to go down the stairs into the cellar and face her fears. Annette also felt that the ghost would like to be rid of the negative memory that is incorrectly attached to him.

We all walked down the steps together into the large cellar space with the dirt floor and the low ceilings. Annette and Diane walked over to the dark corner and talked to the ghost, which only they could see, and explained to him about crossing over into the light, where his loved ones waited. We all watched with goosebumps, as the two psychic mediums described his swirling disappearance.

By the end of the first visit, Annette assured Mike and Miranda that their house was a good house with a good feeling to it. She said that the negative man's energy had sort of been bleeding his negativity into the house, but that now he was gone, they should feel better.

We met with Brian the next week. Brian said that he too believed that the railroad was very, very important to the people back then. Annette previously had said that she was getting a vibe that a young girl had been killed along the railroad tracks toward the town of Readfield. Brian, who knows some of the local history, said that he had heard of a woman whose name was Aida Hayward who was murdered down by the old Belvedere Inn, back in the late 1800s, but he didn't know if it had anything to do with the railroad tracks.

"We didn't have incidences every day there, but you felt at times like you were not alone. I spent more time in here, more than I did anywhere else, and there were times when I was sure that I was not

*photograph courtesy of Mike Ketchen*

alone."

Brian continued: My experiences at the house, growing up, were similar to Betty's, except Betty remembers feeling as if she was being chased going up the back stairs. I was always chased out of bed from my room and down the stairs. I still to this day have nightmares about that house. Not being chased through it, but in my nightmare I am forced to go back into the room. I would have to go through the bulkhead door, with no lights on, across and through the basement, and then I would have to go up the stairway, and over the barn. When I was over the barn, the ceiling would be way up there, like five stories high. That's how the ceiling looked to me, and sometimes I could see up all the way through the floors, as if the floors were transparent.

It was an unfinished part of the house, and that's where the man would come from. He would open the door and say, "I'm going to get you!" I would wake up from my dream, and I would be halfway down the stairs already, trying to get past him. That happened very often.

There was one time that I was sure I was awake; I call it kind of a sleepwalking incident. It was the middle of the night, and the door in the front room was wide open. Outside of the door it was daylight, and it was a beautiful day, and there were a man and a woman standing there with their suitcases.

Brian told us that he had talked to Betty's sister, who at first couldn't remember any unusual circumstances in the house, and then she suddenly remembered that she was walking up the stairs one day carrying a light bulb in her hand, and it just shattered, in her hand, for no reason at all.

Brian gave us a tour of the store, and we went up a few stairs into a small, barn-like space that was used as an office. The space looked like it was virtually unchanged over the past one hundred years. Brian said that his workers often felt something, especially in this part of the store.

Annette and Diane both described seeing a short man and a woman there. They felt the man was a spirit, and they told us that they could see him spinning around in a chair, stating that he was the boss. The woman, who was a ghost, was wearing her work apron, and apparently she thought she was still living back in the early days when the store was the Maxim Feed and Grain store. The man said he had been trying to get her to cross over with him for a long time. Annette and Diane talked to the woman ghost and told her about the light, and said that she should go towards it and be with her loved ones. All of a sudden, as Annette and Diane described to us, the woman appeared as if she was being sucked backwards! While this was happening, her husband was excitedly pointing his finger at her and saying to her, "I told you! I told you!" as she swirled around and faded away! Annette and Diane thought it was a very beautiful scene that was both quite comical and moving at the same time. We all got shivers!

Brian led us through the warehouse at the store which also was the former site of the Paris Farmers Union store. We went up to a large attic space that had very old, exposed beams, and was an original part of the building. Brian said that this was the place that had a very creepy feeling and that Miranda and some of the other workers refused to go up there. Annette saw a ghost, a sad little girl whom she spoke with. She said this ghost told her that she hung around because it was fun playing here, and the ghost said, pointing to Betty, "Just like her when she was a little girl, when she played in the fields around here!" Annette was able to cross her over by describing to her what was going on and suggesting she go towards the light.

Brian said that he would sometimes be working in the warehouse and would hear people walking across the floor or moving around. One of his warehouse workers, who often worked well into the night, would say, "You can tell when you have worn out your welcome!"

"It's not always that frightening," Brian says, "but you just know at times that you are not alone."

He took us through the formal warehouse, where Annette saw a man and a woman ghost, and a few others who appeared to be whispering and talking about us, perhaps wondering what we were doing walking through the lonely old spaces. Annette described seeing a lot of people there who appeared to be waiting for the next train.

Brian said that the trains had gone through here from the 1800s until the 1980s. The grain store was serviced by the train, which transported feed, lumber, grain, and building material.

Annette told us that she could see a lot of ghosts going through, back and forth, and that it was actually like a "vortex" of people. Annette suggested that the people carrying suitcases that Brian saw across the street, at the front of the house, were perhaps coming from the train.

Brian said that they could often hear the large door open, and also that there had been a lot of commotion around the door in general. "The prime time for hearing stuff in the warehouse," Brian added, "was around eleven p.m." He showed us an old swinging door, which had a drawbridge that went out to the train cars. It was a very interesting place, and it certainly had a feeling of the past.

Annette asked if there were passenger trains there, too, and Brian said there had been one named the Flying Yankee. However, he believed the main activity here related to the freight train business. Annette was sensing the activity of people traveling. She said she felt it was not just the store and the house across the street that had activity; it was the entire area that felt rich with vibrations from the past. Annette described a ghost of a man wearing overalls, rolled-up sleeves, and a tweed hat with a little brim around it.

Annette frequently described ghosts as she saw them. "I see a young boy; very thin," she said, "maybe between age fifteen and twenty-two. I'm getting that he is fascinated with your elevator. By the style of his clothes, I feel he is from about the 1920s."

We found both the Ketchen house and the store to be quite amazing, and spooky.

I later heard from Mike and Miranda that they were thankful that Annette and Diane had put the Ketchen family at ease in their home by sending the negative ghost on to the light.

Annette later told me that the negative ghost came to her at her house in Temple and apologized for his behavior!

*Chapter 8*

# Judy and John's Hauntings

*It was Brian Ketchen of Winthrop who had first told me about this haunted house in Readfield, where he had boarded his horse a few years ago and had first-hand experiences with ghosts. I contacted Judy and John, owners of the old farmhouse, and they agreed to share their ghost stories. According to Judy, owner of Mia Lina's Restaurant in Winthrop, the original part of the house was built around 1865.*

The following account was transcribed from a recorded interview with Brian before I visited the home:

We had a few instances over there where strange things happened, like the stall doors would just come open for no reason at all. Judy and my wife Kelly had bought a horse together a long time ago. His name was Smith, and his stall was down in the far corner of the barn. It is a very large barn, built on a slope, with two levels to it. The Morgan horse lived in the lower level, and on the upper levels there was a lot of storage material, and we were helping Judy clean it out. There was a grain room that had a separate door, and it had a very heavy feeling, if you know what I mean.

When people went up to the stalls (most often it was myself doing chores up there), weird things would sometimes happen, like the grain door would fly open. There was an old mannequin in there that they had a lot of fun scaring me with. I used to keep the door shut so I wouldn't have to see it in there, and one time the door just flew open and all the grain went flying out everywhere. Once, I opened the window and climbed out on the roof, which slanted down, so I could climb down that way to get down to the stalls. Well, I had climbed out there, and I realized I had forgotten a screwdriver or something. It was a crankshaft-type window. It was locked. I had to holler for Judy to come let me back in. When I looked at my tools, they were all laid out neatly there for me, and there was the screwdriver, which I know I didn't have when I had come out of the window.

I had another experience at the end of that pasture where we would take the manure in wheelbarrows. I was on the corner of that pasture, and I turned and looked up, and there was a man standing there on the other side of the fence. He said, "You never saw me coming, did ya?!" I just kind of blinked once, and he was gone.

My wife and I used to hear cowbells up here, every now and then, and there were no cows around anywhere. Still, it was a place that has very many good memories for us. It was very peaceful up there.

I visited the home to hear John and Judy's intriguing stories. Annette and her sister Diane came along for the interview, with my daughter Jillian, and me. We sat down at the kitchen table with Judy and John in their lovely kitchen, and the stories began.

In John's words, "We used to have lots of traffic over in the barn, with folks like Pat and Brian Ketchen, who boarded their horses, and they would come twice or three times a day sometimes. Oddly, it seemed like we had quite a bit of activity over there; for example, things disappeared. In fact, it was like a standing rule in the barn that if you took something or used something, you put it back where you found it. So if someone else came, they could find the pitchfork or shovel, or whatever they needed. Then, someone would come along to use the manure fork, or some other tool, and it would be missing. You know, we have peg hooks everywhere for tools to be hung up on. Often, two or three weeks down the road, it would be right there, hanging up where it should be. One time something that had been missing for a while showed up lying right in the middle of the driveway."

Annette told us she could see a ghost. "As you are talking, there is someone standing to your right, and I can see the sleeve of his overcoat or something, and it's like he is trying to hand you something. It's like he is trying to give you something back that he has taken. He is a tall, thin guy, and dressed like he is from the 1800s. He is saying, 'I'm sorry,' and he is trying to give something back to you. It's like, he's the jokester, and now that he's caught, he wants to give it back to you. I think he loves the attention."

Judy told us, "The most recent thing that occurred happened about a month ago. I was cooking burgers out on the patio. I looked up and I saw a flashlight, like somebody was walking with a flashlight across that field." She pointed to the field across the street and below her house. "It crossed the street and went up the driveway by the neighbor's house. About three seconds after, I saw it cross over by the garage. All of the neighbor's lights went out. The house was ablaze with light just before that. I was actually crouching down behind the grill on my deck, watching all of this, afraid he would see me. I'm thinking, 'Should I call my neighbor?' But I didn't see his car. I still called my neighbor, and nobody was home. So anyway, we called the police. The State Police came, and there wasn't a track anywhere in the driveway or in the field! And it had snowed just prior to that."

"It was him," Annette said, referring to the ghost she had just spoken of. "But he is saying, 'Not a flashlight, a lantern.'"

Judy was shocked, "Oh, because it was bobbing...! I said, originally, that it was bobbing. It was a guy, it was definitely a guy, because I saw him and he was wearing long trousers, like a light camel brown, and I could see his coat. It was dark, but I could see his trousers and his coat. He had, not a top hat, but a brimmed hat. He came from across the road, I clearly saw him. It was dark, but I could clearly see him swinging his light." Judy realized that if it was a flashlight she had seen the light would have shown ahead of the person. But a lantern would have shined light around it, illuminating the man's figure as well.

Annette asked, "Is there a lane across the road? He's telling me something about the word, lane." John answered that there was a Lane family that used to own a lot of property which is now Elvin's farm, just up the road.

"That's why it's called the Lane Road up there," Judy said.

Annette said, "It is him. The man is saying it's him who was carrying a lantern across the field. He was one of the caretakers of the farm. He said this was quite a place in its heyday. He is a caretaker, he's saying, and it's like he had to button up everything at night, and there were many acres to this farm and he had a big responsibility. He was like a hired hand on the farm, but also it's like he was family. And by the way, he says he does that every night. He checks on the place every night, he says, and he loves it, absolutely loves it here! Here, you have a watchman, and he's watching out for you," Annette told John and Judy.

Judy admitted that she felt foolish about the incident involving the police, and wondered at the time if she was heading for the loony bin. "But I know what I saw, and I saw that man!"

"He's one of many ghosts here," said Annette, "men and women and children, they are saying. Some are from the house, but they are also from the area. They kind of collect here. 'You guys love us,' the spirits are saying. So that's what I'm getting—that this is a very active place, and it's not just the people from this house, but it is also a neighbor connection."

John and Judy, speaking about the history of the place, said they believed that the house was originally owned by the Nickerson family, and then the Saunders family lived at the farmhouse after that.

John added, speaking about the same incident, "I went out by the driveway one night because I wanted to keep an eye on the property. I would swear on a stack of Bibles that in the upstairs window, in one of those bedrooms, I could see a light moving around up in there. I called the police, but the policeman searched all through the (neighbor's) house, and there was no one there."

John told us about some unusual or unexplained things that happened to Brian and Kelly, and Pat, Kelly's mother, when they boarded horses here in the barn. "There was one time when Brian was alone in the barn doing some chores, and out of the corner of his eye he saw someone walking by the barn door wearing a long black coat. Brian walked over by the door to see who it was, and there was no one around."

Annette said, "It's him again," referring to the caretaker ghost.

John continued: Quite a few times I would go out to the barn, usually around five o'clock, and I would go out and clean the stalls and feed the horses. I would go back out around ten o'clock at night just to check the horses, and I would give them some hay to eat. Once in a while when I went out there, the horses would be all edgy. I would get anxious, and the hair on the back of my neck would just be standing straight up.

Now, one of the times when I went out there, a horse was just walking around loose in the stalls. Judy will tell you that I am always sure to lock and bolt the stall doors. Judy and I really have always thought it had something to do with a woman named Mattie Hackett, who had been murdered on or near our property many years before. The murder was never solved.

"This man liked that gelding," Annette said, explaining that again it was the same caretaker man who she thought was responsible for letting the horses loose in the stalls.

Judy told us that around 1984, a woman came to their door and inquired whether they had any strange things happen in that house. "She said that rumor has it that Mattie Hackett is living in your barn! And I said, 'Who the heck is that?'"

Judy told us the story, or legend, of Mattie Hackett, as she knew it, (see the Chapter 13 story on Mattie Hackett) and related to us that this woman felt that Mattie Hackett was still haunting this area.

Annette's sister, Diane, told us that she felt the stories were mostly folklore, and that Mattie Hackett was not a ghost, nor was she haunting this farm. Annette also acknowledged that she felt that the hauntings in the barn had no connection to Mattie Hackett, and were indeed mostly caused by the caretaker ghost.

Annette was getting a name like "Charles" or "Chapman," in connection with this caretaker ghost. Judy wondered if this was the ghost of a caretaker that she knew of that was on this farm years ago. She said that he was an old man, who went by the name "A.B."

Annette insisted that this ghost really liked John, and was still trying to hand him back something while we were talking about him. Annette couldn't tell what it was, but she said it was something small in his hand. Annette believed it was something metal. Annette asked

John if there was something of his that was missing.

John remembered that he had been missing a small jackknife. "I can't find it anywhere," he laughed.

The ghost told Annette that wasn't it. The ghost indicated to Annette that John had dropped his jackknife somewhere, and that it wasn't what he was trying to hand back to him now. The ghost even added that the missing jackknife was still around. Annette continued to try to guess what the object was.

Annette again explained that this caretaker ghost liked the barn, and especially the gelding, and that's why he sometimes let it out of the stalls.

"Well then, why did he lock me in the grain shed? He scared the crap out of me!"

Judy shared another story. "I was in the grain shed, and there used to be a door on it that we kept bolted, so that the horses, if they ever did get out, wouldn't get into the grain. So, I walked in there, and I heard 'slam!' and the door slammed shut, and bolted by itself! I think I screamed. I had to crawl out the window and jump into the lower barn, and I ran as fast as my butt would carry me to the house! Later John went up to check and sure enough the door was bolted."

Annette told us that the ghost said, "Sorry!"

"There have been other strange times up there, and I learned to carry a flashlight. Once I would turn the barn lights on, I would set the flashlight on the table. I learned to carry a small flashlight in my pocket because, as I learned, once I was out in the barn, quite often it would happen that the light would just turn off. So I would get my little flashlight out, and I would check the lights and the fuses, and everything would be okay. I'd be thinking, what is this? So, we had it checked, and there were no electrical issues. Quite often, the switch would be on, but the lights would be off. A couple of times, I would be in the stall, and I would feel a cold breath or maybe wind or something on my neck. I would be like 'Ooooh!' But really, over time, I've lost my fear about it. But it spooked the hell out of me at the time."

Diane said that there was more than just one person playing games. She was getting that it was a woman causing the lights to go on and off, not the caretaker ghost.

Then Judy half-jokingly said, "Can you ask them who it was that locked my dog, Trevor, in the basement?" She explained. "Well, I got up in the morning, and the kids were getting up, and I said, 'Where is Trevor?' We were looking around and scouring the house, and I said, 'Where did he go?' Well, we have some traveling kennels down in the basement, and so I went down there, and as I walked by one of them, I heard this whimpering whine. I said, 'Here is my Trevor!' He was in the kennel! I have never forgotten that. I don't think Trevor ever got over that either, because I could never get him back into that kennel again."

Diane said "they" were saying, "It's just our way of saying hello." They added that they would never do the dogs or anyone any harm.

John said, "I would go up into the barn, and I would see the horses loose in the stall, and I would just think that it must be Mattie Hackett. I would say 'Mattie, don't do that, because they could hurt themselves.' Then it wouldn't happen again for a little while."

John told us about a time when their son Nick said he woke up in the night, and there was a lady standing beside his bed.

"Oh, yeah!" Judy exclaimed, suddenly remembering it herself, and adding that Nick was probably about fifteen years old at the time. Annette said that she felt this was a grandmother or aunt visiting him, in spirit, not a ghost connected to this house.

Annette said she was getting a feeling that there were children around. She asked if there were any apple trees around the property. Judy said yes, there were a lot of apple trees that went with this farm, across the street. Annette said she was getting that there were children playing in the apple trees, mostly spirits, but some ghosts, too. Annette also thought that there once was a one-room schoolhouse nearby.

When asked if there were any other hauntings, Judy said that oh yes, in fact, there were hundreds of unexplained odd things that had happened around the property over the years. Annette and Diane again told Judy and John that they were experiencing both spirits and ghosts. Judy said that though her mother had passed away about five years before, there were times that she could still smell her perfume around. Annette confirmed that it was her mother visiting her. John added that even at Judy's restaurant, Mia Lina's, in Winthrop, it is not uncommon for even the workers to smell Judy's mother's perfume, Estee Lauder's "Beautiful."

"She had good taste," Judy added. "But not a lot of women wear that. So, when I'm sitting here in the kitchen, and I get a whiff of that perfume, I know it's my mother. And some of those women who work at the restaurant swear that my mother is around. They are completely convinced that she watches over them daily."

We enjoyed our visit at the old farmhouse, and we decided to call David next door, to see if he was aware of any hauntings at his house as well.

*Chapter 9*

# The Old Nickerson Place in Readfield

*David, the owner of this very old house, told us that it has some of the best wall murals in the state of Maine, and indeed, in the whole country. The murals were signed by Jonathan Poore, an artist who was famous for his murals at the time. David thought the murals were said to have been done around 1830. The murals include scenes of hills and houses and interesting-looking trees.*

*The plaque on the front of the house reads "Capt. Dudley Haines, ca. 1790." The Nickerson family lived here for many years. Walter Nickerson, who was born in the house in 1869, married Mary Austin around 1909, and they built the house which is next door and just up the hill, which John and Judy live in now. This house had been left unoccupied for about thirty years after they moved next door. Calvin Norton bought the place around 1943 and fixed it up, but his family lived there for only a few years. Many windows had been broken when he bought it, a chandelier had been stolen, other parts of the house were vandalized, and many antiques stolen. Aley Olson bought this house and the three hundred acres, in 1949.*

*Sitting on top of a hill in Readfield, the house has a feeling of days gone by. The old woodwork, tall ceilings, fireplace mantles, beautiful archways, and many of the other features have been beautifully refinished by David and his fiancée Patricia. At the time of this writing, the house is for sale. There used to be a barn that went with the house, across the road, as well as the attached carriage house and barn that all are now gone, the victims of a very snowy winter in 1944.*

I visited the house twice in two days. David and Patricia invited Evelyn Potter and Beverly Norton Newton, whose family lived here years ago, approximately 1945 to 1948; (her father was Calvin Norton), and I for a tour of the house, and to hear about their ghost experiences. David and Patricia graciously showed us the entire house, which they had recently restored. David said his daughter Meghan always felt there was someone in a little closet space that was in a back room in the upstairs attic space. Evelyn, a spiritual reader and local historian, shared with us some of her impressions about the house. She felt that there had been a fire in the upstairs hallway at some point in the past. Beverly recalled that something about the stairways had made her feel scared as a child. She didn't know why, but they scared her. Evelyn was also getting a feeling that there had been lots of children here in the distant past.

Beverly told us, "I remember being very at home in this old house. An only child, I played throughout the house, and never felt lonely. We never heard anything about ghosts when we were kids. Certainly that was never talked about around children, anyway. But, at the top of those stairs, there was something spooky there."

"You can feel it, going up and down," Evelyn agreed.

We went upstairs to the attic rooms, and Evelyn said, "Whoever used to come up here was terrified of thunderstorms." Evelyn said she sensed that there used to be a little girl who came here and was absolutely petrified. Beverly said that the Nickerson family had a daughter, and she wondered if it was her.

David talked about the recent incident when his next-door neighbors, John and Judy, had seen all the lights come on in his house (see previous story), and a man walking with what appeared to be a flashlight, across David's driveway. David said he had come home late

## The Old Nickerson Place in Readfield

that night, and had turned around in John and Judy's driveway for some reason, and John met him at the end of the driveway.

John had said, "You can't go in there." John told David that Judy had seen someone walking up his driveway and that all the lights were on, and then they all turned off completely.

David said there was no doubt Judy was convinced that she had seen all the lights turn on, then turn off in his house, and that she was certain she had seen the man, and she was quite scared. Soon after he had come home that evening, the state trooper also arrived. Laughing, David said that the house was all locked up, and there were no footprints anywhere around. But he said Judy was completely convinced of what she had seen. "There was zero questioning, in her own mind, of what she had seen," he repeated.

He remembered that Judy had said, "I am not going crazy." David, somewhat a skeptic, said he himself never felt or saw or heard any ghosts in the house, all the years he has lived here. Yet he found this story to be very intriguing!

I came back the next day with Annette to further explore the home. Annette said she felt a sadness when she arrived, and it made her want to cry. She said it usually means a ghost is showing her how he or she is feeling. She felt this feeling came from a male presence. She then picked up on a ghost when she came into the house which was standing in the corner. Annette said that the ghost was telling her that he had lived on this farm, "ages ago." The ghost conveyed to Annette that he missed his wife. "He is showing me a long-handled three- or four-pronged pitchfork. He is wearing a small faded red checkered shirt, and jeans. That's what he's showing me." Annette pondered how far back in time his style of clothes might be.

Patricia said that she and David had just shown the real estate person that day an old article from the 1940s about a man named Thurston. The article was entitled something like *An Officer and a Farmer*. David and Patricia thought this could be the man that Annette was seeing. The article talked about the man's accomplishments as a colonel in the army during World War II, his involvement with NATO, and a story about the fact that he was acquainted with Dwight Eisenhower. The article also mentioned how he had come to live here after the war, and that he enjoyed being a farmer.

David and Patricia said they had just had this article out about two hours earlier, and they were talking about this man with the real estate person, and perhaps this had caught this ghost's attention and brought his presence here at this time. Annette thought that the sadness she felt definitely came from this ghost. She stated that because we were all talking about him, he was now aware that he needed to cross over to be with his dead wife. She said he had a grin on his face, and appeared to be crossing over at that moment.

Out near the stairway, we discussed how Beverly had said the day before that she was always scared of this stairway. Annette said she thought an older lady had fallen down the stairs many, many years ago, and that she had later died from her injuries. She said that Beverly may have been picking up on the feelings of her ghost. Annette said that something upstairs was trying to get her attention, but that she wasn't done looking around downstairs yet.

Later, as we walked upstairs, Annette said she was getting a vibe from a male presence, as well as feelings of a child there, too. She was sure that there was a little girl around, and that she was somehow connected to this older lady who had fallen down the stairs. The little girl was about eight years old, and had blond hair. The older lady and the little girl were from the same time period, and had shared a life together somehow, according to Annette.

We walked by the doorway of a small room, and Annette got the word "sweet" connected to the room. Perhaps, she said, this may have been the little girl's bedroom. David said that this had been his daughter Meghan's bedroom.

As we approached a small door leading to an attic-type space in the back of the house, Annette was already getting something. She had goose bumps. She said someone was trying to touch her, and she asked whoever it was to please communicate with her in some other way.

"Go over there, over there, over there," the ghost was saying to Annette, as if it was in a hurry.

There was a tiny closet-sized room off the attic space. Patricia said that David's daughter Meghan, now an adult, used to go in there as a child, and was terrified of the place. Patricia said Meghan still feels like there is someone in there, and that she had, just last year, gone back into that room just to sit and see if she could still feel the same feelings now that she was an adult. "It used to creep her out," Patricia said.

Annette said, "The man who is communicating with me is not connected to this place, but he is frowning at what happened there. I am getting the words, 'It wasn't right.' Okay, I just asked them if it about punishment. They said yes. Okay... and I feel like crying. Someone, somewhere along the line, used to abuse children and abused this boy. Not the young girl, she wasn't touched. It was a young boy, and I don't know why they were so hard on the boy, but they used to put him in there for punishment, and it's making me very sad. I am aching for this boy, and he died young, too. Oh, they used to beat him, and they put him in there (closet space). I don't know if he died from the abuse or if it was from starvation or what. I am going to tell this sweet, sweet boy that he can cross over into the beautiful light."

Then she said, "I just saw the image of a boy's face flash on the wall over there; that must be him. I am telling him to go find the light, and be with his loved ones, where it is peaceful and beautiful. I hope he hears me. He likes us and he wants to stay with us for a minute. He is not yet ready to cross over. He is happy that someone is acknowledging him and talking to him. He is standing up straighter now, as if getting more confidence."

Annette could then sense that he was ready to go, and she explained to us that he was a ghost who was stuck in time, and that he didn't realize he was a ghost. "I feel like he may come back and thank your daughter; she might feel something sometime, a hug, or just feel really happy. I don't know why, but I think he's going to find her and say 'thank you,' because she made the effort to sit there and find out what was wrong. That is really a beautiful story, and now I'm happy for this boy because he can go on now, and be happy. He was stuck here. That's why this other male presence was anxious, and was touching my back, and wouldn't leave me alone. I don't know who that man is, but he knew about the boy."

She continued. "You do have a lot of ghosts here, but I do hope they all cross over. The man who wanted me to go in this room just said 'Yes, we are cleaning up.' That's what I do, I go into houses and help cross over ghosts, because that's what they need to do to be happy, and go on with their journey. For example, this boy had been stuck in here for years, in his own world, gaunt and starving."

Patty said, "See, Meghan knew."

Annette said, "Now he (the boy) is talking about the farm, and the horse-drawn plows. It seems that he is validating or identifying the era of his time, when this was a very impressive farm."

Patty also added that Juliet the cat always loved sleeping in that closet space. "Out of the whole house, that was her favorite sleeping place."

Annette said the male presence was very playful with her, and was trying to get her to hold something with her hand. She said he seemed very animated, and was trying to be silly or funny, acting almost like a clown. She said to David that she thought he was an uncle of his. Annette asked if he had an uncle who was a comical type of person when he was alive. David admitted that he did have two uncles, Elmo and Buster, who were French, and who were very "fun-loving." David said that both uncles were medics in the war. Buster had died a long time ago.

"Buster was a medic on D-Day, on Omaha Beach. And after he came home, he was never the same."

Annette asked David if Elmo was the funnier one, because she felt it was Elmo, not Buster, who was present.

At this point, Patty laughed, and said, "That is very weird, because David was just telling me about his uncles last night for the first time. He said that they were quite the characters." David verified that they always joked around; and that they always had something funny to say.

"Okay," Annette said, "Then that is who he is, your uncle Elmo. I thought he was a ghost, but he is actually a spirit, and he is here because of you. He is the one that helped release the boy. He has always been with you, and will always stay with you until you pass, he just told me."

"So now that you know this stuff," said Annette, "you need to really try to feel their energy. Try paying more attention, and being more intuitive to your spirit guides. Welcome them. Spirits are very polite (they had very good manners back in their era); but they won't come and intrude on you if you don't want them to. Spirits are very polite, and very respectful."

Annette took a deep breath, and said, "I think your attic is all cleaned up now."

We got a tour next of what David called "The Great Room," a room in the original and oldest part of the house with the original plaster ceiling.

Annette said, "I get a sense of dancing, and groups of people standing around." She said the spirits were saying that it was a nice home, and that it had a nice feeling to it, in spite of the sad story about the boy in the attic.

Before we left, Annette said, "Oh, the man with the lantern is still here. He is making me feel like there is a connection between this farm and the farmhouse next door. He feels responsible to watch over both houses. He wants to stay a ghost, which is fine. He understands everything, and he knows he has to cross over, but he is not ready yet."

*painting by Beverly Norton Newton*

*photograph courtesy of Hannah Faulkner*

*Chapter 10*

# The Elvin Farm
### Story told by Hannah Faulkner of Mount Vernon

During the summer of 1959, before my senior year at Bates College, I lived with my family and worked on a senior thesis in English in the house that is now part of the Elvin Farm at the top of Kents Hill. That house was previously part of the Lane Farm. In 1959, my father, James Faulkner, owned the house and the twenty-acre hayfield beyond. Ten years later, in 1969, he sold the property to the Elvin family.

My mother always liked to keep the windows open to allow fresh air to circulate through the house. Fresh flowers usually adorned a vase on a table in the hallway. In the latter part of July and early August, we experienced thunderstorms almost every afternoon around four o'clock. I remember that during one storm, the front door blew open, and a fireball spun into the hallway, turned around and spun out the door again.

Our old shepherd-collie dog, Sparkle, had died the year before, and was buried under the maple tree out front. My father was working as a mechanical engineer in Boston during the week. My mother, Barbara

Faulkner, was active in the Maine Appalachian Trail Club, making frequent work trips with her friend Jean from Washington to paint regulation blazes on trails leading to mountaintops. My younger sister Martha had a summer job working at The Weathervane Restaurant in Readfield. She served ice cream there from four o'clock to midnight each evening. It was my job to give her rides back and forth to work in the old blue Chevy that was our second car.

Our maternal grandmother, Florence Wilbur, a resident of Boston, sometimes stayed with us that summer. An early riser, she always went to bed at 7 o'clock and slept soundly, so that I felt alone in the house in the evening. After dark I would read, write, and try to ignore noises and footsteps in the attic that alerted me to other presences. I decided not to go into the attic to investigate because of uneasiness about what I would see there. I was always happy to leave at 11:45 p.m. for the drive to Readfield to pick up my sister and bring her home. Martha slept in the bedroom in the southwest corner of the house, where there was a little rocking chair, and I slept in the southeast corner.

A year later, in the summer of 1960, I came home for a weekend with two friends from the New York City residence club where I lived. As Martha was away, my friend Trish slept in her room. In the morning, Trish told me that she hadn't slept a wink all night because "a little old lady was sitting in that chair, rocking and rocking."

In 1969, my family moved to West Mount Vernon to a house where I never felt other presences.

I loved the Kents Hill house. While my family lived in that old farmhouse, my brother Tim had painted a mural of active people on the kitchen wall. Before selling the house, my father took a photograph of it, and then painted over the mural. In the summer of 2011, more than forty years later, Wendy Elvin kindly allowed Tim and me to briefly enter the house. Fond memories came flooding back as I touched the old wooden railing of the staircase. I remembered the beautiful white wedding cake laid out in anticipation of Martha's 1968 wedding reception, and the children at the reception who now are mothers and grandmothers. I remembered my mother's joy at being in the country after living in town for so many years. Most of all, I remember the happy home she created in that house.

*Chapter 11*

# Evelyn Potter Visit

*Evelyn Potter is a local historian and spiritual reader who lives in Readfield and her house is active with spirits and ghosts. I myself had a reading with Evelyn many years ago, and found her to be gifted and intriguing.*

I brought along Annette and Betsy for the visit. Much of our visit involved Annette reading Evelyn personally, as well as reading the house. Evelyn's late husband, an equipment operator, moved this former camp from Fayette, in the 1950s to Readfield. Annette told Evelyn that she felt that there were ghosts here that came with the old camp, as well as ghosts who are here because of the land itself. Annette laughingly called it a double whammy, an expression that Evelyn said she had many times before used "exactly" to describe her beliefs about this house!

Evelyn told us that she has seen many ghosts and spirits at her home. Her late husband also had psychic ability, and she remembers they had both watched a colonial couple walk across the lawn one day, many years ago.

"We were sitting on the porch and he said, 'Oh look! It looks like they're walking over to Sandi's!' We were amazed that we both could see it. That was the last we saw of them. I live here alone now, but I do feel a lot of commotion."

Annette told us that she was also getting a sense of a caretaker or someone watching over this large piece of land, which used to be a farm. She actually felt that this caretaker was connected to the caretaker who carried a lantern, the one she had seen on a previous visit near John and Judy's farmhouse. Amazingly, Evelyn said that this land was not really that far away from there, as the crow flies, and in fact this property was a part of the same large tract of farmland that once belonged to the old Lane family.

Evelyn asked us if we had ever heard the story about the "preaching rock." She told us, "My friend Beverly, along with a Lane descendant, had searched for years over that way for the 'preaching rock.' When the Lane family first moved here, the church preached from the big rock. They searched for four years, looking out in the woods, and in the fields, stumbling over rock walls. One day, they stopped in here to use the bathroom and have a snack. I was going away, so I just told them to please make sure you lock the door when you leave. Well, I hadn't gotten very far when my cell phone rang, and it was Beverly saying, 'You're not going to believe this, but we just found the rock, and it was practically on your doorstep!' Now, I had seen that rock before, and of course I had no idea what it was. It's a shale rock, and it's the same rock, we know, because someone had a picture of it. The Lane family came over to see it, and took pictures of it."

Annette said that she could see a ghost who wears a long dark coat attached to the rock. She wondered if it was John and Judy's caretaker ghost, because he also had worn a long coat.

Evelyn continued to tell us, "The Lane family, when they first settled here, built a house nearby on the property. They claim that John Lane was the first in that family to come from Massachusetts. He came and built a cabin and planted some corn. Then he went back to Massachusetts to get his wife, and by the time they got back, the Indians had burned it down. There is still a dip out there where the cabin used to be. There's also a ceremonial spring near here. It has been said that the Indians felt that the water was sacred, and they used it as a ceremonial place. There is a lot of history here. You can feel it, especially when you go outside, and especially at night."

Annette agreed that this place feels very active with spirits and ghosts. Annette said that her spirit guides were telling her to look out the porch window, and that out in that direction it was very active with ghosts. Annette actually felt that her guides meant that the activity was the view where you looked out this window, when this cabin used to be in Fayette. Evelyn added that this cabin used to be set way out on a back road somewhere, off Route 17 near Camp Winnebago.

She also told us about a female ghost that appears sometimes, floating over her bed, which startled a visitor who saw it while sitting in her living room one day. "That visit was cut short," Evelyn added with her dry humor.

As we visited and talked about the history of the area, I asked Evelyn again if there were any other hauntings that she could tell us about, at the house.

"Oh, my husband and I always felt like there was a lot going on here. It felt like we always had a lot of company around. I remember one night I woke up, and he was talking to someone, and I said, 'Who are you talking to?'

"He replied, 'Oh just Mother and Phyllis!' He said, 'Can't you see them? They are right here at the end of the bed!' It was his sister and mother, and I said, 'Oh that's great, that means they are together!'"

I told Evelyn that I thought it would be so wonderful, and so very comforting, to be able to talk to loved ones who have passed. Evelyn explained, "Oh, I think everyone can; you just have to accept it."

Evelyn mentioned that her home relaxes and calms people who come into it. "People come in here all in a commotion about something, and when they leave they always feel better." I have to say I really did feel very comfortable and relaxed during this whole visit.

"It has a very good energy to it," Annette agreed. "There is something about the porch, especially, and it's definitely a very active place."

"We sit out there a lot and visit with company, and even at night it has a nice feeling to it, listening to the night sounds."

Evelyn said. "Before my husband was operated on for cancer, in 1983, I woke up out of a sound sleep one night, and there was a person who I think was a male spirit. He had a turban around his head, and he was working up and down on my husband's body as he slept. I watched this healer as he worked, and after a few minutes he disappeared. My husband had cancer of the stomach, and the doctors removed three quarters of his stomach to eliminate the cancer. The doctor said that if he made it through a year without cancer, he would be in remission. Well, he did, though he had four more surgeries. He lived another twenty years, and died in 2003. My daughter Dale felt that this man with the turban prepared him for the surgery, and perhaps even healed him at the time."

Evelyn also told us about a couple of other places in Readfield where she had seen ghosts. The old Asa Giles homestead on Main Street, she said, was haunted by ghosts from the Victorian age. Years ago, she had had an opportunity to go into the house, and she heard old-fashioned music, and saw ghosts dressed in beautiful gowns, dancing ballroom style, from a time many, many years before. She said it was awesome.

She also recalled years ago being in the old Giles brick building, also on Main Street, which is now used as the Town Hall. It used to be an old schoolhouse, she said, and she remembered being able to faintly hear voices of ghost children there. She said that since the building had been renovated, she no longer can hear them when she goes in to conduct town business.

An interesting visit with an interesting lady!

*photograph courtesy of Ellen Bowman*

Chapter 12

# Thunder Castle Hill

It may interest some to read the history of Thunder Castle Hill before reading the owner's ghost story. The following comes from a book entitled *My Notebook of Interesting Old Houses and the People Who Lived in Them*, by Alberta V. Chute. It reads:

"Every village has a mysterious, deserted house, which someone is bound to label "haunted." Thunder Castle, they say, was such a place in Readfield. Only the old cellar is left now, on the west side of Thunder Castle Road. A thick granite gatepost is standing beside the driveway. I was told that it was not here originally, but was bought as an antique somewhere else and moved to this location for a hitching post.

Thunder Castle, or Castle Thunder, as it was called earlier, is featured on the Bicentennial quilt made by Readfield ladies in 1975. The late Dorothy Lanctot, who made the Thunder Castle square from a snapshot taken in 1920 (see above), wrote that the house was L-shaped and was built on Settler's Lot number 230 in the early 1800s. Note the cleared fields all around, which are now covered with trees and bushes.

On the 1856 map of Readfield, M.S. Bean (Manley) is shown on the spot. In 1879, C.C. Bean (Charles) was living at Thunder Castle. Located on a high hill, once called Burnt Mountain, above the east shore of Torsey Pond (Greeley Pond), it must have been an imposing structure.

The old cellar is a small well-rocked-up depression that was under only part of the house. At the north end is a square pile of field rocks with a big flat stone on top, which must have been the foundation for the chimney and fireplace, as evidenced by the pile of tumbled bricks in back. You can see the rock outlines of sheds to the north of the house, and foundation stones for the large barn which was southwest of the house.

You can walk down to Torsey Pond from this highest point of land on Thunder Castle Road. Your trail lies over a winding wood road, spongy underfoot, with lovely trees all the way down, down, down to a big gravel pit, beyond which is Torsey Pond. You can see houses on high Kents Hill opposite, and small houses on a dirt road in the valley between the gravel pit and the east shore of Torsey.

It is uphill all the way back, of course, so you go more slowly. You may find the old yellow birch tree, which is so big that two persons reaching their arms around the trunk cannot touch each other's hands, leaving about an eighteen inch gap between. That makes the circumference somewhere around eleven and a half feet—quite a tree.

On the way down and back, you pass by a huge boulder. It used to be in a mowing field, but is now surrounded by small trees. Mrs. Lanctot, who was brought up in a house on Thunder Castle Road, wrote that the children of her day would climb on the big rock and holler across the open field, and the echoes would reverberate like thunder.

Some say the house itself was built mostly on ledge (which would account for the small cellar), and when there was a thundershower, the noise resounding from the ledges was terrific. The elevation—five hundred and forty feet, according to the US Geological Survey map—is called Castle Hill. A little way to the south on Thunder Castle Road is a farm known as "Castle Hill Farm," once owned by the Huntons, and now owned by John W. Tyler.

The Huntons, or Huntoons, owned considerable land in this

area. George Hunton was the son of Samuel and grandson of Peter Huntoon, one of Readfield's earliest settlers, whose name appears on the early survey map on Settler's Lot number 159, which is quite a way to the south of Castle Hill.

Peter is buried in a tomb in his own private cemetery, called the Huntoon Cemetery, located near a crossroads where dirt roads from Kents Hill, Sturtevant Hill, and North Wayne come together. This old graveyard was cleaned out and repaired during the Readfield bicentennial years.

Henry Hunton, son of George, sold the Thunder Castle property in 1930 to Mrs. Irene Chase, owner and operator of Chase's Camps on Torsey Pond. Mrs. Chase had the badly deteriorated buildings torn down in 1932. Roy Mace was the owner in 1959, and he sold thirty-five acres to Dr. Meta Haldeman, a retired psychiatrist, who had a brick house built by Roy Giles, southwest of where Thunder Castle stood.

When Dr. Haldeman died, the property went to her friend and mentor, Dr. Carl Bowman, whose grandson, Richard Janesco, lived in the brick house for several years. The current owner is Ellen Bowman, another grandchild of Carl.

Thunder Castle seemed to attract unwelcome visitors, as such houses always do, and it became known as "Tramp's Retreat" during the years when tramps wandered up and down country roads as well as city streets. The neighbor's geese meandered into the house, and delighted in eating the plaster off the walls (was it the lime they craved, I wonder?).

The "thing" which you can see hanging on the door (see above picture) is the skeleton of a crow, put there for a bad luck sign, perhaps. Certainly, bad luck continued to plague Thunder Castle until it was finally taken down. What a shame somebody couldn't have bought it and fixed it up before it was too far gone. Castle Hill is a lovely place for a house."

Ellen Bowman invited me to her home on Thunder Castle Hill. Ellen's friend Melanie Lanctot was also present, and she shared some history with me, as she has lived just down the road all her life. There are many stories about the property and the old house, which was built on a large ledge of granite on the top of the hill. Melanie's mother had known Dr. Meta Haldeman, who built this house in 1962, as mentioned in the above account. Dr. Haldeman made quite an impression on Melanie.

She said, "Dr. Haldeman was a free spirit before it was fashionable. She never married, and at the time when our mothers were wearing blouses with Peter Pan collars and high heels, she was wearing muumuus and flip-flop sandals. She was an ardent naturalist, and she shared her passion for birds and astronomy with me and my neighbor and best friend, Olive Louise Bishop."

Described as a naturalist, she was obsessed with birds, astronomy, and nature. Dr. Haldeman, thought to be intuitively attracted to this property, was a retired psychiatrist who moved here from Washington, D.C. Ellen said that when Dr. Haldeman died from leukemia, this house was left to Ellen's grandfather, and Ellen then acquired it from her grandfather's estate, when he passed away in 1978.

There are many stories about Thunder Castle, and the unique property, Ellen told us. For example, she heard that when it thundered outside, the house would echo, and that the granite increased the echo. She remembered that there was a man who lived in the house who had many wives, and that he had a very deep voice which sounded like thunder when he spoke.

Ellen, an expressive therapist by profession, says that she is a very spiritual person by nature, but had never had any "trans-spiritual" experiences before.

She shared these stories: This experience really grabbed me. But I really believe that this happened. So let me begin with my former husband, who was cutting down trees with a chainsaw on the property. We were trying to be very careful, and respecting Dr. Haldeman's attitude. It was a brand-new chainsaw, and the chain broke on two different occasions. He had to keep replacing it, and yet we didn't really think anything of it at the time.

Then there was the incident about the cat. I had a locally adopted, really cute orange tiger cat. I think he was about eight months old and not fully grown. He was completely healthy, but apparently just plunged to his death in the bathtub. I just heard this thud, and went in there, and just said, "What?" He had probably been walking around on the edge of the tub, and appeared to have just keeled over and died.

He was just dead on the floor. I wrapped him up and took him to the vet, and the veterinarian said he had no explanation for why the cat would have died.

The other story I have happened when my son was about four years old; this was around 1983. Several times, I would be washing dishes in the sink, and my hands would be in the water (a conductor of energy, I have heard), and I saw what I call a gray peripheral blur coming into the kitchen door to my right. The first time it happened, I just thought to myself, oh you are just tired. The second time I just thought, oh it's just dust, or dirt.

Then my cousin, whose name is Arthur, was studying for his Boards, to be a lawyer, and had come to stay here because he needed a quiet place for a while. He came and stayed for a week, and upon leaving he said thanks to me for giving him a place to study for his Boards.

Then he said, "Oh, by the way, I just want to tell you that this funny thing happened when I had my hands in the kitchen sink, doing the dishes. There was this gray peripheral blur that came in the kitchen door!"

He used the same exact words to describe what he had seen as I had thought to myself about what I saw! I had kept this to myself. I thought, "Holy moly, this is real!" So it was just a confirmation for me. My cousin had also told me that he had experienced hearing his name being called here a couple of times, when no one was around. I never had an audio experience here.

Then, as things happen in Maine, events go around by word-of-mouth. I was swimming laps at the YMCA in Augusta. I was pausing between laps, and a man beside me in the next lane was also taking a breather, and we started talking. I found out that he was a serious student of the famous psychic Alex Tanous. I guess we were talking about where we lived, and I shared a story about this house, and he said, "That is fascinating. I want to get Dr. Tanous to go out and do an assessment of your home." Well, sure enough, he arranged the assessment! He came out the next week. It all happened because of him and our encounter.

And so this famous psychic scholar, Alex Tanous, who was world-renowned because of his predictions, came to my house. This man was very busy and really brilliant. He had had an extra sense, and had done many investigations, and talked to many spirits from beyond.

He came here in June that year, and tromped around the grounds and read the whole history of Thunder Castle. Now, there is a huge glacially made rock ledge, which even for me has a spiritual quality, and he made note of that. He asked all of us questions: my husband, my four-year-old son, and I. It was all very reassuring, and he told us that there could be reasons why we were having visitations here. He said that he felt that Dr. Haldeman was not residing, but overseeing with loving protection and endearment. He felt that she was sort of caught between two worlds, as she had built this house and loved it so. There was nothing to be afraid of, or concerned about.

He said the reasons that spirits visited the living were: that they could have been just visiting, or perhaps there had been a terrible injustice such as a murder, or it could have been that a person had died a tragic death, and that there was a message that was incomplete; or finally, he also said it was possible that a spirit could visit for the purpose of protection. He felt in this case that Dr. Haldeman was just being protective.

He said to us, "You are her caretakers, and you are living in concert with her wishes. She approves of your life here, so do not alter your lifestyle."

He asked if my four-year-old son had mentioned her, and suggested that she watched over him closely and would sometimes enter his play. Children are just naturally psychic, he said, because they have not learned to build up layers of protection as they grow. They are just raw receptivity to the world, he said, and they are naturally spiritual.

Alex Tanous told us that Dr. Haldeman was intuitively drawn to this place, and not by accident. He said that there are also Native American roots here, and that there are remnants of healing, as in a medicine man spirit. He felt that it was a Native American meditation ground. He said that if you went digging around here, you might find remnants of the Native Americans. He told us that the information he gathered here would go into a record of his investigations, and I believe either his widow or his daughter runs the Alex Tanous Foundation and website, where this information might be found.

## Chapter 13

# The Mattie Hackett Story

There are old-timers in this area who still remember the story of Mattie Hackett, a young woman who was murdered in Readfield years ago. When we visited John and Judy's farmhouse, they told us they had only lived there a few months when a woman came to their door and asked if they had any ghosts. This visitor told them it was rumored that Mattie Hackett "lived" in their barn. Judy and John had never before heard of Mattie Hackett.

Judy said she'd heard the story like this: "Originally, there was a second barn attached to our barn, to the left of it, and close to the road. Evidently, Mattie Hackett, who was sixteen and married, went to the barn one evening after supper, and she saw her husband there with another woman, and she shot them both dead. The last time she was seen, she was on horseback, riding down P. Ridge Road. That's the folklore of this town. So this woman told us that she believed that Mattie Hackett was haunting our barn!"

Because I had heard about Mattie Hackett being connected to this property, I had brought along a copy of an old newspaper article which was found online. According to the article, Mattie Hackett was the murder victim and her murder was never solved.

The article stated that on August 17, 1905, a pretty woman named Mattie Hackett, the daughter of a respected farmer, was strangled to death near her home. The story was that she was doing dishes after supper and was for some reason called out into the yard. She was later found unconscious by the side of the road near her home and it wasn't noticed until her father had carried her into the house that a cord had been wrapped around her neck so tightly that it was embedded in her neck. She reportedly died before they could cut the cord away. A local woman named Elsie Hobbs Raymond was tried in court during the highly publicized murder trial and found not guilty due to lack of evidence. At a time when murders in Maine were mostly unheard of, the very notorious murder trial focused on rumors that Mattie had been spending time with Mrs. Raymond's husband and that the woman had killed Mattie in a jealous rage. Mrs. Raymond maintained her innocence through the entire trial.

Annette and her sister Diane were with me during this visit and upon hearing the story, felt that what really happened was much different than what was written in the newspaper article. They immediately felt that the facts in the story itself didn't jive. Annette and Diane, who were able to get information from their spirit guides, immediately felt that the Raymond woman was not responsible for the terrible deed. Diane's guides were telling her that the information in the newspaper article was "small talk," and had been embellished by the newspaper reporters. In fact, they both immediately felt that Mattie's father was the murderer. Diane's spirit guides were hinting to her, "You don't accuse a prominent man of murder, now do you?"

As we explored further, Diane told us that Mattie Hackett's father was angry with her because she had a boyfriend. Immediately, Annette got the strong feeling that Mattie's father had been molesting her. "The father was jealous, and he was sick, let's just put it that way, and she had fought him off that night."

"Yes," Diane added, "Mattie had put up with enough abuse, and so she tried to defend herself. Buried, dead, and dirty secrets."

Annette added, "Her father was afraid that she would tell someone, so he killed her. But, Mattie is not a ghost; she does not roam these hills."

We visited the farmhouse next door a couple of weeks later with Evelyn Potter, also a spiritual reader, and the subject of Mattie Hackett came up again. Evelyn said that she too always felt that it was Mattie's father who was responsible for her murder.

Now, as everyone knows, rumors fly like the wind, and there are many stories out there, and much speculation as to what really happened to Mattie Hackett. As for me, I feel like I have the inside scoop from my psychic friends.

*Chapter 14*

# The Walton Farmhouse

*Anne and David Sinclair live in the old Walton farmhouse in Wayne. Here is Anne's story as she related it to me.*

We moved into this house in 1974. It is in the history books as being built around 1830, and it is described as, "A very nice farmhouse on a hill overlooking a fine trout stream." The couple we bought the house from had lived here for about twenty-five years. As everyone around here knows, Evelyn (Walton) Randall grew up in this home. Evelyn had given me all of the history about the house and the Walton family. For example, there is the story that a surgery was performed years ago, right on the kitchen table. Evelyn told me that someone had pneumonia or something, and that the doctor had to open up a lung right there in the kitchen.

Like many old farmhouses, there was a birthing room right off the kitchen, where it was warm from the kitchen woodstove. I asked Evelyn one time if there were any ghosts in this house, and she said no, that the people who lived here were serious and hard-working people.

Anne continued: When we first moved here, Dave was working all kinds of strange hours as a trooper with the State Police. At that time in State Police history, they were on call twenty- four hours a day, seven days a week. Even when they had days off they were still on call.

Our first son was born in 1975. Our baby Michael and I were often here alone at night. That was fine, but then I started hearing noises. It would be quiet at night, and the baby would be in bed, and that's when I would start hearing the noises. I would be thinking, "Okay, I am definitely hearing something..."—and it was always around the area of the chimney in our bedroom. The sound I heard was more like a whispering or a rustling sound. It was not like the sound of the wind going through, or an animal caught in the chimney. To me it was a definite whispering sound.

At first when I would hear it, I thought it sounded like someone was trying to tell me something, and it was like a breathy sound. It was a female voice, and it was actually very comforting. I never ever felt any fear. It was like I knew that she was saying it was okay that we were here. It was always like she was trying to have a conversation, and it seemed like she was always just drifting around.

Our second son, Matthew, was born in 1977, and Dave was still patrolling. Sometimes when Dave was home, I would ask him, "Don't you hear something?" or "Don't you hear something around that wall where the chimney is?" He would say he didn't hear anything, or "It's just the wind." He was always trying to find a rational reason. But I choose to believe it is a ghost, and I choose to believe she is friendly, and I choose to believe she lives in this house and everything is fine!

I called her Beatrice, but I'm not sure why. I asked Evelyn Randall about all the people who have lived in this house, and there was no reference to a Beatrice. I guess it was just my own thinking where I got the name, or perhaps it was an old relative of mine.

Then we did renovations, and we worked on the two front parlors in the house. In each room there was a mantel, even though there were no fireplaces behind them. There were woodstoves in those areas. We were just unearthing those walls that were bad. We were also tearing out the ceilings to expose the hand-hewn beams, and in that process, opened the wall that was under the ceiling beneath our bedroom. That was the chimney where I had heard the noises.

We found some interesting things inside the wall. We don't know how they could've gotten in there unless somehow there was a crack or space near the mantle at some point in time, where things had fallen into the wall. We found a small pair of glasses with a case, a child's shoe, some coins, some newspapers, and some very tiny pictures in tintype frames. They have gold and brass around them, and they are very ornate. Two of them are of a man, and one is of a woman, which was unusual at the time because generally only men had portraits done.

So I asked Evelyn Randall if she knew who these may have belonged to because, of course, I was infatuated with them. If these belonged to her relatives, she would want them. She said they were not her relatives, and they were no one whom she recognized, so she didn't think they belonged to anyone who had ever lived here. The Fogg family had only been here since about 1950, and these were much older than that. I choose to believe that the little picture of the woman is Beatrice.

After we had the renovations done, the sounds went away. I don't know if there was a natural reason, like a draft that was in the chimney which was now filled up or something. I don't know. I also had the thought that maybe the ghost may have been hiding between the floors, not in the chimney! It was definitely disappointing when it stopped. I missed hearing her. It was a very real presence, and it was as if she knew that we were in the house, and it was all fine.

*Chapter 15*

# Sally Towns' Ghost Story

*Several years ago, Sally and Nelson Towns lived in the old Norris place in Wayne, which Sally believed was haunted. A no-nonsense kind of woman, I was surprised to hear that she believed in ghosts. Here is her story as she told it to me:*

T "The first experience happened when we had only been there about two years. We had completely gutted the house. We had rebuilt the house, even moved it from a dirt foundation back onto a full foundation. We had our first exchange student come, and she was from Mexico."

One day we were coming home after I had just picked her up at Maranacook School, and we came in the driveway. We had a horseshoe driveway, so we came in on the left side where there is a bay window on the front of the house. Both of us saw the curtain in the window go back, as if someone was looking out to see who was coming. Vicki said, "Oh, Tom must be home."

Tom spoke up and he said "Huh? I'm in the back seat!"

89

So she looked at me and I looked at her, and we knew Nelson wasn't home. She said, "Ahh! It must be the cat!"

I said, "Yeah, it must be the cat." So, we went on in the house. After a few minutes, we knew the cat wasn't in the house, and a few minutes later, there was the cat, outside! It had come to the door and wanted to come in. So, we had no idea what it was.

These strange things always seemed to happen with the exchange students around, and I don't know why.

Then there was the time when we had Roberto living with us. This one night Roberto and Tom and I had been sitting up and watching a movie. Then we all went to bed. The boys were a little wound up; Tom was about age eight or nine then. Anyway, I woke up, and I could hear voices. I could hear something like a conversation going on downstairs.

I thought, "Oh God, those kids are up." So, I went downstairs—the stairs are to the left of my bedroom, and the boys' room was right across the hall from me. So I looked in their bedroom, and they were both in bed. I thought, "Did I leave the television on?" I wasn't sure, so I went downstairs. Nothing; it wasn't on. So I went back upstairs and went to bed. I had just turned out the lights and closed my eyes, and again I could hear voices. It was like a conversation, though I couldn't hear what they were saying. It seemed like two or three people having a conversation down in the kitchen.

After that, I heard footsteps. To explain, when you came upstairs to go to the bedrooms, you would go around the corner and down a little hallway, and then it turned and went up to the bed fold, which was up in the attic. In the old days, that's where the help would sleep, if they had hired farm workers or whatever. And there were peg hooks, where they had apparently hung their things to dry.

So I could hear the footsteps coming up the stairs, and of course this time, I'm panicking because I'm thinking somebody is actually in the house. Well, I lay there very quietly, and I heard the footsteps just turn and go down the hall, and then they went up the other stairs. I could actually hear them go up the other stairs! I got up, and there was a basket of sweaters that was sitting at the bottom of the stairs, and I knew it was there earlier because I had been cleaning out a closet that had a cedar lining in it. When I got up, the basket was still sitting on the bottom stair. There was no way somebody could have gone up the stairs without moving the basket. I quickly went back to bed, and covered my head with the covers!

There were other little things that happened all the time. Many times things were misplaced, and I'd be looking everywhere, and then whatever it was would appear on the counter, or somewhere that you wouldn't have missed seeing it in the first place. Weird. It was nothing bad or scary really, ever. The ghosts were friendly, and it was as if they just co-existed with us. I think they were happy that we had redone the house.

Another time I remember was when another exchange student, Miguel, was with us. Vicki, another exchange student who had come back for a second time and was with us for another year, was watching television. Miguel and Tom had gone up to bed. All of a sudden I heard Miguel say something, and I didn't know what it was. Then we heard this thud, thud, thud, thud, thud! Well, he had fallen all the way downstairs! He was kind of sitting at the bottom, and he looked at me and said, "What!? What did you want?"

I said, "I didn't want anything, I think you are sleepwalking!"

"No," he said, "you came right in, and you woke me up, and said I needed to come downstairs!" Now, he could have been sleepwalking or dreaming, but even days afterward, he was adamant about it. "But I'm sure it was you," he'd say.

When my mother came to stay with me, before she passed away, we had the television room fixed up for her, and she had a bell she could ring when she needed me. One night she started ringing the bell, and I went in. She was wide awake, and she said, "That man was here again."

I said, "What?"

She said, "That man was here again."

I said, "What man?"

"I don't know; he just sits here." She pointed across the room and said, "He just sits there in that chair." Well there's no chair there. But she insisted she saw him sit down there.

I said, "Well what does he do?"

"Nothing, he just sits there."

"Is he watching out for you?"

"Maybe."

About four nights later, she rang the bell again and said, "That man is here again." Now, whether it was because she was coming to the end of her life, or whether she was actually seeing something, I don't know. She saw it, no matter what. She died a few weeks later.

That was it, other than the regular stuff. One of the Norris brothers built the house. It's an old, old house. One of them lived here all his life with his family, and the house got added onto as he lived there. It started out with just one big room downstairs. The story was that his wife passed away and his family was gone. Things started to degrade, and the barn fell down. There were chicken houses, and they fell down after a while. Over the years, it just deteriorated. I think he was probably there for thirty or forty years by himself. He had a housekeeper and that was it. When he died, she had to move out. I heard he didn't pay his taxes, so the town took the property after he had died. I think he probably died in the house, but I don't know for sure.

*Author's Note: Sally very sadly passed away in October 2012 just before this book was to be published. She was a wonderful and generous lady who is missed by all who knew her, including many local children who fondly called her "Nana Towns."*

Chapter 16

# The Old Cottage in Wayne

*It has long been rumored by locals that the Old Cottage in Wayne is haunted. Though no specific stories could be nailed down, it has been reported to be a mysterious place where strange noises have been heard. The Old Cottage was built in the early 1900s by a wealthy man from out of state named John Carter. He summered there with his wife, Elizabeth, whom he doted upon, and in fact, her name is immortalized on a fireplace hearth. A desk, which still remains in the camp, also bears her name, carved in the wood. The Carters were reportedly friends with Thomas Edison, who supposedly may have visited the Old Cottage. The camp has changed hands only three times since the Carters, and it remains very much unchanged since the early days.*

We visited the Old Cottage in Wayne on a lovely summer day. Mary and George Ricker are the new owners who bought the historic place in November of 2009. Suzanne, Mary's sister, graciously agreed to a visit. Though they hadn't yet experienced any strong ghostly happenings, they welcomed us to come and to explore the cottage with psychics Annette and Paula.

Paula immediately saw a male ghost, and described him as dressed with a navy blue jacket and matching low-brimmed hat. This ghost told Paula that he was here when the cottage was built. This ghost told Paula that "Everything was for her (Elizabeth)." We looked around at all of the furniture, original to the house, including John's and Elizabeth's carved antique desks.

As we talked and looked around, Paula saw the male ghost in a mirror, and she said he was laughing. She felt he was a friend of John and Elizabeth Carter. Paula asked him what Elizabeth was like, because the man kept saying to her, "It was all about her (Elizabeth)." The ghost added, "He, (John) could have done better...!" Paula said she was getting the impression that this man was not so fond of Elizabeth. "He deserved better," the ghost said. Clearly, John doted on Elizabeth, as evidenced by the personal touches throughout the house, her name imbedded in the fireplace, and her name carved into her desk, and so on.

Annette was also getting the words "sea captain," apparently from a ghost who also explained he was not from this camp, but he had stopped by to say hello. Annette felt the place was very active with spirits and ghosts.

Upstairs in the very cozy camp, we walked through the rustic and cozy bedrooms, and Paula told us she saw a woman on the bed, which we surmised was Elizabeth's bedroom because the desk with her name carved into it was in this room. Paula said she saw her ghost lying on the bed, and heard her say, "Get out!" to us. Paula described her as wearing an old-fashioned nightgown. After a few minutes, Paula surmised that this ghost was not feeling very well.

Annette heard someone say, at the same time but in another room, "She doesn't feel very well." Annette didn't know who the voice was referring to at the time. She thought that it was the man in the blue jacket who had said this to her.

Annette spoke with the man who confirmed that indeed, he and Elizabeth didn't get along. The ghost again reiterated, "Everything was all about her, and everything was for her."

Annette walked into the bedroom and apologized to Elizabeth for our barging in. She told us that the ghost spoke to her and apologized for speaking rudely, and again validated that she wasn't well. She told Annette that her husband was very sweet to her and that the other ghost was merely jealous of the attention that her husband gave to her, and also the money that her husband had. She said she and her husband were very much in love with each other, and so her husband spoiled her. Annette said Elizabeth said thank you and kissed her on the cheek!

Back downstairs, Paula saw another ghost wearing light blue overalls, an older man who she felt was the caretaker. This validated Annette's earlier mention of seeing the same ghost.

As we were preparing to leave, Paula saw another ghost, a little girl, who was skipping from the screened-in porch and down the catwalk that joins the cottage and the boathouse. She looked at Paula as she went by. Paula said she was wearing a dress that appeared to be from around the 1920s. The ghost told Paula that she was from "over there," pointing down the lake. She explained sadly that she had drowned, many years ago, after she had slipped off a ledge and fell on some rocks and into the lake. The ghost indicated that she often came to the Old Cottage just because she liked it there. She skipped off and disappeared just as quickly as she had appeared.

It was an awesome experience to tour this very unique cottage, and we thanked Suzanne for her graciousness in allowing us to visit the ghosts and spirits for this book. The place definitely gives one a feeling of the past. As we drove out of the driveway and were riding by the cemetery, Annette saw more ghosts, of a man and a woman, among the headstones. We were fortunate to experience another haunted place in Wayne!

A year later, someone told me another story about the Old Cottage.

I met an interesting woman who is known to her friends as Flaun, at her annual antiques sale at the old Mill Stream Grange building in Wayne. Flaun sells antiques for a living in California, but has summered in Wayne for years. Flaun, whose grandfather was a shaman, has some psychic ability as well. The following is her story about the Old Cottage:

A couple years ago, I got a call from one of the neighbors, who knew the owner of the Old Cottage at the time. They wanted to know how much their furniture was worth. So I went over there to do an appraisal on their furniture. They showed me the downstairs, then we went upstairs, and there were three bedrooms and a bathroom. I was writing down on a piece of paper what I thought the total appraisal was. Then the guy started to go downstairs.

I said, "Don't you want me to go in that other room?"

The door was closed, and he said, "No there's really nothing much in there."

I said, "You know, there may be the most valuable piece in there."

And he goes, "Well, if you want to go in there, then just go ahead and look." And he went ahead and went downstairs, which I thought was kind of odd.

So I went over and opened the door, and the minute I opened the door, I just got blasted with this energy! Every hair on my body stood up on end. I said, "There's a spirit in this room!" I was drawn to the bed, but I didn't actually see anything there. I think the spirit in the other room had to be a different spirit, because it was definitely the wife of the man who owned it for some forty years.

So I felt the energy, and I said, "Hi, I'm just here to look at the furniture!" All of a sudden I just felt washed over with this vision of what had happened to this person. I got the impression that the cottage had been purchased for her as a wedding present from her husband, and that they used to go there and stay all the time. One day she was carrying something, and she was on the steps and lost her balance, and she tumbled head-first all the way down the steps. She hit her head on the wall at the bottom of the steps, and died from her injuries. At the time I just tried to shake it off, and I said out loud, "Whoa, that's why you stay here."

When I came out, I went downstairs and I spoke to the people again. "So, that's why you don't go into that room, because of the spirit."

They said, "Oh, we don't know what you're talking about. We just don't go into that room."

I said, "Well, obviously it could be used."

I could see that it was all dusty and had cobwebs everywhere, bat droppings, and everything. I said, "It's because there is a spirit living in there of someone who died in this house."

"We don't know what you're talking about," they replied, because at the time they were trying to sell the cottage. I don't think they wanted the story to get out. So we just left it at that.

Well, about a week later, I was in here at the lodge, having a sale, and there were people in line waiting to check out, and I was telling someone I was going to put an offer in on the cottage, and I said, "Yeah, I think I can get it cheap because there are ghosts in there!"

This lady standing in line was listening, and she said, "What do you mean there's ghosts in there?"

I told this woman the story I've just told you, and when she got up to the line she said, "How did you know that story, about the lady?"

"Well, the spirit had told me in whatever way you get that kind of information," I said, "because the story passed before my eyes. But I'm really not sure how it happened."

The woman looked at me and said, "That was my grandmother, and nobody outside the family knows this story."

As far as the appraisal went, Flaun said she recommended that the family not sell the furniture, as it was original to the cottage, and Flaun felt it was not right, or even necessarily lucrative, anyway, to sell it. So thanks to Flaun, the original furniture still remains with the cottage.

A little follow-up story: just recently Annette told me she had listened for the first time to the recording we made of our visit, though it has been well over two years since we visited She told me that she could clearly hear a voice in the background, like a high-pitched old lady's voice, saying, "Get out!" in the background of the recording. Spooky!

*Author's Note: The owners of the Old Cottage decided they did not want to scare their summer guests, and so this story has been disguised with fictitious names.*

Chapter 17

# Wayne UFO Stories

*There were some UFO sightings in Wayne one particular night in the mid-1970s, and Linda McKee, a correspondent for the Kennebec Journal at the time, wrote a story for the newspaper about them. I am not one who necessarily believes in UFOs, but hearing the following stories made me really consider the possibility. Though there were more reports that night around Wayne, this UFO sighting was, in fact, reported by Linda's next-door neighbor Mike Waitt. Here is his story as he told it to me recently:*

Our family lives on what used to be called North Pond Road, now called Walton Road. One weekend I was walking from my house up towards the field where the horse barn was. My parents were in the horse barn at the time, and I remember it was nice out. This thing came from the north direction, heading south, and it came over the trees and over the field. It seemed like it kind of hesitated over our house, and then it took off in the direction of Berry Pond. I ran into the horse barn and told my parents about it. There was a neighbor of ours, Ronnie, who was there, too.

We went into the house, and I remember we all noticed there was an electrical smell throughout the house. For the life of me I can't remember the year or exact date, but I was probably eleven or twelve years old at the time. It looked like a saucer, and it had these glowing, spinning lights all around it. When it left, it left quickly! I mean, when it took off, it was like nothing I had ever seen before. There was no sound—it just kind of came over the trees and over the field, right over my head, hesitated over the house, and then just took off! I can still remember it all, and the smell in the house, like an electrical wire had burned or something. It was something else! To this day, what amazes me was that there was no sound to it; nothing at all.

Linda McKee wrote the following account:

I was a correspondent for the *Kennebec Journal* at the time. That's what they called us. We covered specific areas in Kennebec County, and I got paid by the inch of text in the article. The day after the article appeared in the KJ, a second sighting was called in by a woman on Fairbanks Road. She said she had been sitting on her porch overlooking Berry Pond that same night, and suddenly saw a bright flying object streak across the sky. She said it coincided time-wise with the Waitt boy's sighting.

The evening of the Waitt event, Roy (Mike's father) arrived home while his son and wife were up in the horse barn talking. Before he knew anything about what had happened, he immediately called us here next door to ask if we "smelled anything funny." He said the smell was "Sorta like Freon," and permeated the whole place. He wondered if something had gone awry with his freezer. I received the call, and said that no, we smelled nothing unusual here. He called back later after hearing his son's story to ask me to come up and interview him for a story for the newspaper. I recall distinctly listening to the boy's story, thinking he was not making this story up. He told it quietly, evenly, as though almost in shock. It was not a story coming from an overly imaginative child who had gotten carried away. I had four young children at the time, and I knew the difference. He was telling the truth.

Soon after hearing this story, Jackie, a woman who lived at that same time on the Cross Road which is across from Berry Pond, told me this story, and I wondered if it was the same night:

My mom and I saw a UFO in front of the house one time. We had just moved there, and we had no draperies yet, and my mother and I were sitting on the couch, looking out the window. We saw this huge UFO right in front of the house, right in the street! It was getting dark out and we could see this circular thing just hovering over the street.

Mother and I just looked at each other, and we never told anyone about it. We had just built this house in 1975, my ex-husband and me, so this might have been about 1976.

When asked what color the object was, Jackie thought for a moment and she said, "Kind of a pink, and it was huge, huge, huge! Bigger than a house, it was humongous! We just stared at it, and about an hour later, we just looked at each other, but we couldn't say anything, because anyone would think we were crazy! So of course, we didn't tell anybody about it for a long time, because no one would have believed us.

My mother and I never talked about it. I remember I went out the next day and looked in the street to see if there was any mark or anything. There was nothing there.

Here's another story told to me by a well-known local woman from Wayne who chose not to be identified:

It probably happened in the summer of 1974 or 1975. I was walking back from my friend Ruby's along the Pond Road on a summer night. As I approached the elementary school, a bright blue light moved along the treetops in back of the school, flared, and disappeared behind the trees. There was no sound at all; the whole thing probably only lasted three minutes. I walked home very quickly, very scared! It was so strange and nothing like I had ever seen before.

Because these stories were reported to have happened in the mid-1970s, I have to wonder if the people in the above accounts all saw the same UFO on the same night. The stories are eerily similar. I do know that each person who told me their story seemed sincere and convinced that what they saw was real.

*Chapter 18*

# The Underwood House

*Known as "The Underwood House," Sarah and Bill Reed's brick house in Fayette is both beautiful and historic. It was named after the original owner and builder, Joseph Underwood, who was born in 1783. He built the house in 1836, and it is said that he inspected each brick himself, rejecting many. He was an accomplished man, and was involved in local and state government. The house is rich in history and has many unique features, such as a "cooling board" in the attic, which was used to keep a corpse cold until spring, when the ground was thawed for burial. The original board still lies across two beams high in the attic. (See back cover picture.) A slaughter room in the cellar, for pigs and chickens, still remains, and has an open brick fireplace with a large kettle hanging over it, which also adds to the spooky vibe.*

The following was transcribed from a recording of Sarah Reed talking about her experiences in the house:

The first thing I can tell you is that my grandfather had a sense of knowing, and my mother pooh-poohed the whole thing. She wouldn't have had anything to do with this. She thought it was strictly of the devil. She was German, and was raised in a very fundamentalist church. I have since changed very much. My daughter, and my son who died nine years ago, both seem to have had that sense, especially Danny. So before we came to this house, we had already experienced some things.

The first time I came here was in the summer of 1992. I went to the Echo Lake Association, and they introduced me as the new owner of the "Brick House," and a few men from the community came up to me and said, "Welcome! You know, your house is haunted!" I laughed because I thought they were trying to scare me.

So I just said, "I'm sure it is."

They all looked at each other and laughed, and they said, "We all know it is!"

I just ignored the whole thing because I really thought they were trying to scare me.

Nothing happened around here until June of 1995. That was the first time that I was actually aware of the spirit. That night I was here alone. It never dawned on me to be scared. I went upstairs to bed. Sometime during the night, I woke up. I realized that I was covered with something black; it was black, dark, and evil, and I wasn't sure if I was going to be murdered or something, but I knew I was in danger.

Before that, I had had another experience in which I really called on the Lord in prayer, so I hollered out "Jesus, Jesus, help me!" and when I turned around, the room was empty. It was the middle of the night, but I was completely shaken as I felt there was something evil there. That was my first experience with this spirit-thing.

That was in June. In December, we were here for the holidays. My son Dan had gone to bed. During the night he said he felt this blackness, and he reached out to knock it away. He said he called out to me, but you don't hear well in this house because the walls are very thick. But the next morning he came downstairs and said, "I can't sleep in that room anymore. There's a spirit there. She's the one who did all the flower beds."

In the middle of July, one night I was asleep again alone, and I heard this banging. My neighbors had been working on their house, and I thought, "It's late, so why are they doing this?" All of a sudden, I raised up a little bit, and in the corner I saw this old lady dressed in a long skirt and white blouse, and an older man who was banging with a hammer. Whether she was helping him or watching him, I don't know. They were working, and it was like looking at a mural. You know, you see everything. I couldn't touch them, but they were there.

I said, "For God's sake! It's two o'clock in the morning, keep quiet!" And that was it. I was curious, but I was also tingling. I think it was old Joe and his wife, since they were dressed in old-fashioned clothes.

That August, I had our minister come here to do a house blessing, and the prayer was that no evil or dark spirit would be allowed here. But if they (good spirits) love this house as we loved this house, they were welcome. And since that time I have been startled, but I have not felt threatened at all. So I guess it worked. There are a lot of crosses and angels here, because I decided we would have a cross or an angel in every room.

One night, it was either right before or right after this, I had just crawled into bed and turned off the lights when I heard someone walking in boots. All I could think of was those boots that men wear with big heels. I heard a man walking up the steps.

I said to him, "It is okay, we're here now; we're going to take care of the house." The steps stopped, and I sat in bed for a while waiting for him to go down, but there was not another sound. I definitely heard footsteps on the wooden steps. The next morning, I told Danny, and he looked at me funny. We have carpet on our steps. That was the most real and most frightening thing.

In June of 2003, the son of the previous owner and his wife came back to visit. He visits his mother's grave here. She and I were talking in the kitchen, and she said something like, "Are you Christian?"

I said, "Well I try to be."

She said, "Do you believe in spirits?"

"Since I've lived in this house, yes, why?"

She told me about a time when her daughter had been visiting here. She was about sixteen years old. The daughter was sleeping in one of the bedrooms, and she woke up absolutely freezing. The room was freezing. She put on a blanket. She could not get warm. She thought there was something dark there.

She wondered if we had had any experience like that, and I said,

"Yes, we have."

In June of 2005, I was reading in there, and I heard someone walking in the hallway. Now, it's a big house. We usually keep the doors locked when we're home. I felt like I was being electrocuted. It started at my toes and went right on up, and I couldn't talk, but I knew someone was coming. I realized it was my son, and his spirit was around. I felt his energy.

Sarah also shared with me a note from a woman who had recently visited the house for a social meeting during which there was special piano music. She herself had an unusual experience while she was there. The following is her note as written:

"Dear Sarah, Just a personal note to say thank you. And a second thank you for the summary about the psychic's visit. It had confirmed what I had sensed. It was as if, when the music started playing *You Light Up My Life*, we were joined by spirits coming from all directions. They gathered at the doorways, not entering the rooms, for fear of changing the atmosphere that had been formed. I got the sense that, not only were there Underwoods present, but also some who had a direct connection to the instrument being played. The emotion I sensed was sheer joy, and I appreciated the musical notes that were long missing in the home. Oh, this is like it used to be! Thanks for an incredible experience."

I visited Sarah a second time with medium clairvoyants Annette and Paula, which was very interesting, and revealed more about the hauntings in the house. They certainly felt the house was very active with spirits and ghosts. Though I lost my recording of this visit, Sarah and Bill's daughter, Cynthia Reed-Brown, was also there, and wrote the following notes, which summarized this visit beautifully:

From the driveway, Paula noticed a teenage girl looking through the screen of the upstairs window. She was a plain girl with a plain dress and with her hair pulled back; not a modern girl. From the front of the house, she saw a teenage boy, older, about seventeen, tall and thin with a white shirt and wearing glasses, and looking over the south middle window. She said they were maybe an older brother and younger sister, cousins of the Underwood family. They mostly stayed upstairs because they didn't want to bother the people living here, who mostly stayed downstairs. They liked to play upstairs and run from room to room. The girl really loves the front bedroom, which is the southwest window. From the front hallway and the living room, both women saw a white male servant who seemed to be checking to see what everyone was doing. (We think later that there were no white servants there, but they did have servants.) We think the man was the caretaker, because he did live in the house with them. In the downstairs library, there was a male presence.

In the music room when Annette took pictures from the door, a man looked up at her. He was in the room with a lot of other people who said, "Hi!" He seemed to say, "Oh, you are taking pictures!" He was a more modern-looking, medium-built man, who knew what a camera was. He wore a dark suit, had a receding hairline, and was in his fifties to sixties.

In the parlor "they" said we were supposed to sit, and to sit here. They told Annette to look out the window and into the garden, and twice she did this. In the dining room, Annette said there was a man sitting at the head of the table, a very important man. He stayed seated, and had brown eyes and mutton-chop whiskers. Annette didn't think originally that it was a formal dining room. "The dining room was at first the kitchen, when they were still building the house I am sure, but they would always use the dining room.

Annette thought that the downstairs bedroom, which we always called the Nanny's room, was the birthing room, just because of the size and its proximity to the kitchen. Both Annette and Paula said that there was a good feeling in the room. Now, the kitchen is like a sitting room and a kitchen, and when the Underwood family lived here, it was one big kitchen. In the back room, which was the summer kitchen, there were no particular feelings. except the spirits told Annette that the inside outhouse was originally away from the house because the smell was so bad in the summer. Annette asked about a barn, and thought it might have been on the west side of the house.

There was an older lady at the top of the stairs, heavyset, a typical old-fashioned lady in her nightgown and cap. Annette thought she was probably the mother or grandmother of the first Underwood wife, Mary Aiken. It also could have been the mother of the woman who lived here before. "In the upstairs bathroom, the words 'diary of a female' came to me," said Annette.

In the sitting room, or children's room, there had been some kind of altercation or fight in that room; Annette saw an older man holding a boy by the collar and shoulders and shaking him and saying, "Hey, Hey!" and pushing him around. It was nothing devastating or particularly violent. And the boy was innocent of whatever he was accused of. Also Annette picked up four orbs in the room on her digital camera.

In the back room, which we call the dollhouse room, Paula saw a little girl with straggly brown hair, very unkempt, about five or six years old, who said, "Mine!" when we entered the room. She was kneeling; her face came to the top of the table with the dollhouses on it. While she was playing with the dollhouse in the back corner, Paula asked her if she lived there and she said, "No." She probably plays with the other kids when they are there—our grandchildren.

In the attic, no particular feelings except that Annette's spirit guides told her to look out the window toward the garden again. She asked about the area around the arbor. That's where the previous owner is buried. Sarah told Annette and Paula about the cooling board, and Annette immediately said, "Four women and two men."

Sarah responded, "I have gone through the files, and can pretty much tell you who those people were, because of the timing of their deaths. In those days, if you died after November, you didn't get buried until spring."

Cynthia's note ended with these comments: "In the basement, there was nothing in particular, except that Paula felt sick to her stomach when she approached the middle room, which has always been known as the slaughter room because that's where they killed the pigs and the chickens." That was the write-up of the visit with Annette and Paula.

Sarah continued to explain, "The man that Annette saw peek around the door when we first entered was probably the caretaker, who was reported to have slept in the library. The important-looking man at the head of the dining room table, who looked pleasant but who didn't rise when the women walked in, could have been Governor Kent, because he did come to dinner here. I have a wonderful story about the new dishes that Mr. Underwood bought for the occasion. In fact, I have fragments of those dishes. The only thing was that in a picture I have of Governor Kent, he did not have the big mutton chops. Her mention of the male presence in the library is true, because I have in that room some of my son Danny's ashes, because that was his favorite room."

Sarah said she felt Annette and Paula were the real deal.

Finally, I want to include here the following interesting story which was written about this house, for the 2009-2010 book *People and Places and Their Memories of Fayette, Maine*, published by the Fayette Historical Society in 2009-2010:

"Our family vacationed on Bodge Island, Echo Lake, during the summers of 1938 and 1939. The island was not available in 1940 and 1941, but we were able to rent the large brick Underwood home in Fayette from the grandchildren of the original owner. The grandchildren were Joseph, Mae, and Emma Underwood.

The home was not only very interesting, but intimidating for our family of four. One reason was there was no electricity in the home. When asked about the lack of electricity (although it was on a pole in front of the home), Uncle Joe Underwood stated, "If Grandfather didn't need it, we don't need it." They also did not have electricity on their farm just down the road.

We walked around carrying kerosene lanterns in the evening. Our family stuck close together, especially when we needed to use the indoor outhouse. This was located at the farthest point to the rear of the house.

There were several things that stand out in my memory of our wonderful stay in this home. There was a stuffed owl sitting on a chest at the top of the front staircase leading to the second floor. What was unusual about this owl was that its head was loose and bobbed when anyone climbed the steps. Picture this while climbing the steps in the evening with a kerosene lamp casting its shadows.

Another item of note was in the attic. Two very smooth long boards lay across the rafters. We understood those to be "cooling boards." They were used during the hard winter if there was a death in the house (or family). The body was placed on the board until the weather would allow a grave to be dug and they were able to proceed with a proper burial.

The creaky floors, kerosene lamps, "cooling boards," and the owl with the loose head all created wonderful memories.

**—Written by Dave Shearer,**
age six or seven during the above years.

*Chapter 19*

# The Old Stinchfield Place

*Debbie Swasey, a lifelong "Wayner," is a hairdresser in Winthrop. Among her many Wayne stories, she remembers a mysterious incident from her childhood days on Androscoggin Lake.*

I was probably thirteen years old, and the Lawrence family had just bought the old Stinchfield Farm. I was there with my friend Rose. They were having a party one night; an adult party. Rose and I, and a couple other girls too, were all outside. I remember there were some lights on outside that evening and it was a clear night. The stars were out, and we were just sort of hanging around. All of a sudden, we saw this cloud thing over by the barn. It just kind of kept moving slowly. There were no clouds, and I know it wasn't smoke because it was summertime and we were outside. It was like a mist, and it just kept going across the yard, and then it just disappeared. It was nothing like we had ever seen before, and there was just no explanation for it. We were looking at it and it scared us, so we went into the house. We talked the adults into coming outside to look at it. When they all came out they just kind of stood and looked at it. They said, "Oh, you girls, its fine. It's nothing at all."

Later that night, we could hear the adults talking downstairs inside the house. There was little insulation and you could hear their conversation easily. They sounded concerned because even they had no idea what the apparition was! It seemed that the adults were scared too, but they didn't express it in front of us because they didn't want to freak us out. Whatever it was, it made such an impression on me, and it still gives me the creeps! I will never forget it.

*Chapter 20*

# Cheryl Bennett Ladd Story

*Cheryl Bennett Ladd, formally of Wayne, told me this beautiful story she entitles* Send Me a Sign-If You Can…

It's a beautiful sunny morning, and I'm hanging freshly washed whites on the clothesline. My eyes are drawn to the word "Jesus" on my crisp, white nightgown. The word is a faint charcoal grey in color but clearly visible, and stops me in my tracks. The name Jesus is less than half an inch in length and the font is like one would find in a Bible scripture.

In a bit of a daze, I motioned to my husband who was mowing the lawn to turn the mower off and come over to the porch railing. As he walked up to the steps, I asked him to look at the nightgown and did he see anything?

He said, "I see the name Jesus."

As magically as it had appeared to me, it was soon gone completely from sight.

That evening as I marveled at what I had seen, I was taken back to a conversation I had had with Nana Vera, my grandmother, a few days before she passed away.

I was sitting with her in the nursing home lobby, and it seemed I could almost step into her beautiful brown eyes. It was as though the love and warmth of her spirit was welcoming me to have a conversation of what was to come.

We spoke of heaven, and she sweetly asked if I thought she would see Grampa John when her life here had ended. I told her I was sure that she would, and wanted to know if she was frightened—she peacefully said, "No."

We sat in silence for a short while, and then rather lightheartedly I said, "So, Nana—since it seems like such a mystery, send me a sign—if you can."

*Chapter 21*

# The Wing Cemetery in Wayne

Annette and I visited the Wing Cemetery one day to see if we could find anything interesting going on there. According to Annette, though, ghosts rarely reside in cemeteries. The Wing cemetery is an historic and unique cemetery, designed in concentric circles, each one an ordered generation of the Wing families, who were early settlers in Wayne. Much has been researched and written about this interesting cemetery by the fabulous local historian Eloise Ault, in the Wayne Historical Society's book, *A Happy Abundance*.

We walked around and read some of the inscriptions, and Annette, as you might guess, picked up on some sad feelings, and she said that there were many sad stories that went along with the cemetery.

"They are saying some people have more money than others… I'm getting someone asking what we are doing here!" A few minutes later, "They're correcting me and saying they are not 'markers,' they are gravestones!"

I asked Annette out of curiosity if she got anything from the gravestone with the name "Emmeline." Annette said she was getting a sad feeling, and she noticed that the woman had died at the young age of thirty-six years old. Annette's spirit guides told her that Emmeline had died during childbirth. Annette said she also got that the cemetery was not just a concentric design because they were a close family, but instead that it was because it was a foreign idea. According to Annette, the circle idea came from a different culture, which the designer got when he was traveling in another country.

Several weeks later, Annette and Paula and I were driving by the Wing cemetery again, and we pulled over to the side of the road for a minute.

Paula saw a ghost, and this is what Paula wrote of our visit:

We stopped outside of the Wing Cemetery. As we pulled up in front of the cemetery, I could see a young blond man sitting on top of one of the headstones. He was sitting on his hands with his feet dangling down. He didn't belong to this particular cemetery, but he liked going there. He came over to the small wrought-iron fence and leaned over onto it, and as he looked into the car at us, he said, "It's going to be ok; it'll all work out." I asked him if he belonged there and he said no, he came from "that way," and he pointed down the road in the direction we were going. He said he had been in an accident; a really bad one.

When I'm with Paula and witnessing her as she sees ghosts, I get this wonderful and surreal feeling. I truly believe she is seeing what she describes to me. She and Annette are both very amazing and gifted!

*photograph of Charles King courtesy of Paul King*

Chapter 22

# Paul King Stories

*Paul King is a co-owner of Knowles Lumber Company in Winthrop, and a well-known local character. He approached me one day, and said he heard that I was collecting ghost stories. He told me that ghosts talk to him. The following is transcribed from a recorded visit:*

My father Charlie used to go flying all the time, and my parents were renting the old Waitt house on the Coolidge Road in Wayne. My mother was pregnant with my older brother, and, of course, they didn't know that it would be a boy. My father had four sisters, so there was no one so far to carry on the "King" name.

My mother said that my grandfather, Charles King, used to rub her belly and say, "That's my little grandson!" He catered to my mother, and helped her through it because my father was gone much of the time.

Well, my grandfather died about two months before my brother was born, so he never did get to see his grandson born with the "King" name. My mother said that about two years later, in February 1969, I had pneumonia. My Grandmother King, who lived on Main Street in Wayne, came to stay with my mother because she had recently had a heart attack. My father was off flying, and my mother had my sister, my brother, me, and my grandmother to tend to.

Well, she came down the stairs one morning and walked into the kitchen, which had windows that overlooked the lake. She looked out the window onto the driveway, where her car was parked alongside my grandfather's Land Rover, which my father was using. She looked out there and saw my grandfather! He had his hand on the trunk of the Land Rover as he was leaning on it, wearing his brown hat, which looked like one he would wear to church, and his long brown trench coat. She said she saw him as plain as day! Interestingly, she said she could see him in full color and everything, but he didn't have any feet. He was just standing there looking at them all, and my mother said it made her feel at ease. She said she felt as if, "Oh, I'm not in this alone. There's somebody here looking after me."

She always said that my grandfather never got to see his grandsons, so he was just looking after his wife who had just had a heart attack, and their children and grandchildren. So that's my story, which happened in Wayne.

Now, I have never seen a ghost myself, but they talk with me. My girlfriend Dawnn's husband was killed in an accident, and we got together about a year and a half after he passed away. She was living on Holmes Road in Winthrop, and I was living there with her.

The first time her husband Joseph appeared to me was when we first started going out. It was wintertime, and I was working on a snowmobile. It was actually his snowmobile, and his daughter wanted to ride it. I decided to go out and fire it up. She was out riding it around the backyard, and as she came by, it was making all kinds of noises.

I said, "Oh Lord, bring that over here. You can't ride it like that; I'll fix it." I was working on it in the garage, and cutting some sliders that the track slides on. I had this old hacksaw, and I was hacking and sawing, hacking and sawing; the blade was horrible. I was struggling.

Now, I had never seen her husband before, nor ever spoken to him. All of a sudden I heard this voice say, "There is a hacksaw over there in the drawer." I looked up and looked around, and I thought," What?"

I start hacksawing again. And then I heard, "There's a saw in the drawer, dummy!" So I threw the saw down on the floor, and walked over to the drawer and opened it up, and there was a brand-new blade in the drawer! I put it on and I cut right through it the first time.

So that was my first encounter. I'm thinking, "The neighbors are going to think I'm crazy over here talking to myself!"

The next encounter was about a month later. Dawnn's husband had an old pickup truck that she had kept, and it was backed in close to the garage. When we pulled in the driveway, the pickup truck was facing us, and Dawnn's daughter was next to me in the front seat, and Dawnn was in the backseat for some reason. Well, I looked at her and she was just sheet- white. I'm thinking are you okay? I thought she was sick or something she was so white.

She said, "My Dad."

I said, "What about your dad?"

She said, "He's right there."

I said, "What? I don't see him."

"He's sitting in the front seat of the pickup truck,"

I didn't see him. But she saw him. I said, "Oh Lord."

The next time it happened I was in the kitchen doing dishes, and I went to open the junk drawer. I was looking for something, and I was fiddling around in the drawer, and I found this biohazard bag. I thought, "What is this?" I flopped it out, and Dawnn said, "Oh that's Joseph's stuff from the hospital." The bag had his wallet, his wedding ring, some change; everything he had when he was in the accident, in this little bag.

She said, "Well don't put it away; I want to look at it." She opened it up and dumped it on the counter while I was doing the dishes. I could see she was messing with something. I heard this ping, ping, wing, wing sound and the wedding ring is spinning around and rolling on the table. So I looked at that, and as I said, I had never met the guy. I'm thinking to myself, hmmm.

I didn't say anything out loud to anyone else, but I was thinking I wanted to try that ring on and see how big of a guy he was. These are the thoughts that were running through my head. I hadn't spoken to anybody. So I left the kitchen sink and walked over, and I reached my hand out like this (he out stretches his hand), and I got the weirdest feeling in the world, and I thought, "Oh Lord." I pulled my hand back, and I thought, naw, this can't be, it's all in my head! I reached for it again, and I got closer this time; I got an even weirder feeling!

I told Dawnn, "Your husband is here. And he doesn't want me to touch that ring!"

Then I said, "Okay, Joseph, I won't touch it."

Dawnn said, "Who are you talking to?"

I said, "I'm talking to your husband." He didn't actually talk to me this time, but his message was crystal clear. So I thought, okay, let's put this stuff away.

I think it's kind of cool. I've heard a lot of stories through the years about people seeing people who have passed away, and things that really don't make any sense. People are back and forth about whether there's something after this life. There are just too many instances that I've seen and been involved in to not believe that there's something else. It's frustrating sometimes, because the people that I'd like to talk to who have passed away don't talk to me. Just because I have business to settle with them doesn't mean they have business with me. I don't understand it all, but I'm certainly open to it. Now when I hear these stories, I think, "What? You saw them? Really?" I'm very intrigued by all of it.

*Chapter 23*

# Camp Androscoggin Ghost Tale

*Tom Lane of Wayne shared this ghostly tale, which has been passed down for years to campers at Camp Androscoggin in Wayne. Tom, whose father worked at the camp for many years when he was a child, had his first job there when he was just fourteen years old, mowing grass and bailing out boats. When Tom returned to Wayne in 1970, he became the Maintenance Director there for twenty-five years.*

In the early 1940s on the island at Camp Androscoggin on Androscoggin Lake, the chef for many years was Jimmie Jett. Everyone loved him, but he had one disconcerting feature, and that was that he had a glass eye that didn't turn with the other eye. He became famous for it. Eventually he died, not during camp season but in New York City, and no one claimed the body. The story was that if someone claimed the body, they had to pay for the burial. So the Director at Camp Androscoggin claimed the body. He had the body cremated and brought the ashes, which were in a paper bag, to

Camp Androscoggin. Well, he had set the paper bag down on a table outside, and there was a sudden downpour. The paper tore and the ashes formed a little pile, and on top of the pile was the glass eye! As it continued to rain, the glass eye dislodged from the top and rolled down the side of the pile of ashes, and disappeared.

So the story is that at night when you hear what many people think is a branch rubbing against the screens of the bunkhouses, the counselors explain to the children that it is Jimmie Jett, looking for his glass eye!

*Chapter 24*

# Mysterious Footsteps in Wayne

*David Criss believes in ghosts, and he told me that his parent's house in North Wayne, where he grew up, was surely haunted. All the years growing up, and until the recent passing of his parents, Ry and Laurel Criss, David's childhood home had a ghost. Here is his story:*

The house was built in 1848 for the managers of the North Wayne Tool Company, which was down in the town, and once spanned across the stream where the dam is today. They built these houses for the management people. In fact, if you look at the neighbor's houses, and my parent's house, the basic design is the same. My parents bought it in 1947, and it had been a summer house for a while for some people prior to that, but I can't remember their names.

My ghost story is this: where the front door is, there are stairs to the upstairs where the three bedrooms are, and at the top of the stairs is a loose board. It has been that way since my parents bought the house. You could hear somebody walk back and forth and you could hear when they stepped on that board. It seems like sometimes it would be every night, then it would go away for a while, and then it would come back. You would be sitting down in the kitchen or in the front room, and it would be all quiet, then you'd hear it.

When I was a kid, we didn't have television. We might have had the radio on most of the time, so people would be reading or playing card games or board games. So again, it would be quiet, and then you would hear somebody step on that board. You'd hear the other footsteps and then you'd hear the board creak, then you'd hear more footsteps. As I said, there would be times when you wouldn't hear it for a while, and then you'd hear it several days in a row. That's the only thing we ever heard. Whatever the aberration was, it didn't seem to be malicious; it was just there. It was part of the house.

It was kind of neat, because we'd say, "Oh, whoever it is, is here tonight!" We never named the person; we didn't know if it was a male or female, a child or adult or what have you; it was just there. It wasn't a bad feeling either, because you felt like you weren't alone. You were in the house, and well, most people might feel creeped out. We never got creeped out because there was never anything associated with it that made us uneasy. In a sense, it was our Casper, the Friendly Ghost.

I was raised here, and now it's where I will spend the rest of my days, now that it's mine. Since both of my parents have passed, I haven't heard the noise at all. I don't know if the ghost or aberration has crossed over, or if the familiarity is gone, I don't know. It was nothing exciting, you know, you won't get people in there with "ghostometers" or "ghostbusters" or anything like that (he laughs). It was just an interesting thing to have. Again, it was just a friendly, even comforting feeling, an "I'm not alone" kind of thing. So that's it. It's just basically a simple story; and an interesting phenomenon of the house!

*Chapter 25*

# Three Pine Farm in Readfield

*Everyone in town knows Julie and Ian Cundiff, the friendly owners of the Wayne General Store, but most people probably don't know that Julie and Ian own a haunted house in Readfield. Recently, they shared their spooky stories. Julie began:*

My ex-husband and I bought this old house in Readfield, about sixteen years ago. It needed a lot of work. It was all torn down in the back. It had no plumbing or electricity. There was one bedroom from which you couldn't even see out of the windows because it had so much stuff piled up everywhere. Everyone told us to just burn it down, it was so bad. But I could see the potential in the house, so we bought it. When we bought it, one side of it was basically a barn. It had a summer and a winter kitchen. It was in this old barn part that my ex-husband saw the ghost. We always called those parts "the old side" and "the new side."

We had another house in Belgrade, and so the Readfield house was just a project. We got started and did a lot of work. One day my ex-husband was in the old side of the house. He was leaning down and picking things up, because there was a lot of old junk, but there were a lot of good things, as well. As he was leaning down he could see, out of the corner of his eye, a guy standing there. The guy had a baseball cap on and a flannel shirt. My ex-husband said, "Oh, hold on, we'll be with you in just a minute," because the neighbors would frequently come over and see what was going on, because the house had been abandoned for so long. No one had been in it for about two years. He stood up after he put down what was in his hands, and looked up, but the guy was gone. He went outside and looked around, and nobody was there.

We went up to the Jesse Lee Church about two weeks later, and met some people, and we told them where we lived. They said, "Oh, you live in that house? There is a ghost in that house!" Of course, we were thinking, "Pease don't tell us that!"

It was then that we tied the two together, and knew that the guy my ex-husband saw was a ghost.

At first, I was really afraid of the house, because it was just creepy-looking. Then I got more comfortable, and we started staying there. Eventually, we sold our house in Belgrade and moved into this old house at Three Pine Farm.

One night I was working on the computer, and I was really intent on something. All of a sudden, I felt this chill go right up my back, like there was someone right behind me! I looked, and there was no one there. Nothing. For a few seconds, I was thinking that it must have been the ghost. I thought, "We have been here for a while and the ghost hasn't hurt anyone, and he is probably glad we have fixed up the house for him."

Time passed, and my ex-husband and I were divorced. I met Ian, and eventually he and I got married, and we lived together in the house.

Ian continued the story: The house was really divided in two, and so we decided to open up the other side. I went ahead and cut a hole in the wall that went to the other side of the house, and I was just sitting at the table. I saw someone walk through from the other side of the house and into the living room, with a baseball cap on, and I thought it was my son.

I yelled, "Josh!" and he didn't answer, so I got up to go talk to him. There was nobody in the other room. Other times I would be just sitting in the house, and I would hear sounds. Sometimes it would sound like children running up the stairs.

Julie explained: We did some research on the house, and had tried to do some genealogy on it. Someone said that a lot of the information was lost because the town hall, or wherever they kept the records, had burned down. We found out later that someone was murdered in this house. We learned that by researching online, and found an article written about the murder, which took place in the 1950s.

The story was that it was the farmer who had owned the house. His hired hand had wanted a raise or something, and the farmer had said no, that he wouldn't pay him any more money. The man left, and then he came back through another door and went upstairs. He knew where the farmer's shotgun was, and he went upstairs, got the shotgun, and shot and killed him. He dragged him down into the basement. There were pictures in this newspaper article, and there were blood stains going across the floor and down the stairs. The body was in the basement for three days before anyone discovered it. There was an investigation, and they soon found the hired hand somewhere outside the state and arrested him. So we think that the ghost is probably the farmer who was murdered here. We honestly feel he is a nice ghost.

Ian joked, "He hated me! Everything went wrong for me in that house!"

"Yeah, okay, the house has been kind of a nightmare for us!" Julie added, laughing.

Julie also said. "We actually made it into a duplex, and we rent it out, now that we live in Wayne. We put a floor in over the opening to the basement. We were uneasy about the spirit or something down there. The only access to the basement now is through the bulkhead."

"Yeah," Ian said, "The basement is very, very creepy."

Julie added, with emphasis, "It really, really is."

Ian said, "It's horrible down there. The stairs even broke one time on me. You really feel like someone is watching you down there. And no one will go down there with me. Devon went down there once, and then quickly took off. A water pump was always corroding all of a sudden, and I had to go down to fix it a lot. Many times the cover would be on, and so I'd go down there, and it would be just tossed off. Really weird. I hated going down there."

"My daughter, Brelyn, felt a presence in her room once," Julie said.

"The house is really old, and dates back to 1778. We know that because we found a beam with that date on it. A lot of prominent families once lived there. The Dudleys, and also the Governor of Massachusetts once lived there. I am sure it was a beautiful house back in its day."

*Chapter 26*

# Readfield Historical Society Visit

*A story in the local newspaper about a paranormal group visiting the Readfield Historical Society building in Readfield revealed rumors of ghosts there. Florence Drake, President of the Society allowed us to visit to see for ourselves. Annette and Paula, who are always happy to come along and explore a haunted place with me, came to see what they could pick up on. It's so amazing to hear what they see and feel from their spirit guides!*

The following account is taken from Paula's journal, which she wrote later that day.

Annette and I went to Cathy's today for a little ghost hunting. We arrived at her house first thing in the morning. We went to the Readfield Historical Society. I asked my spirit guides, or I should say I told them, that if I am meant to see or hear anything at all on these visits today that I would accept them as they came and I wouldn't question them.

130    *Hauntings from Wayne* | Cathy Cook

*photograph courtesy of Readfield Historical Society*

*photograph courtesy of Readfield Historical Society*

At the Historical Society in Readfield I saw a boy sitting at one of the desks. There were a number of desks in the room; some of them were double desks, but the majority of them were single desks. The boy had dark hair and very dark eyes, almost black. He looked like he was horsing around with someone sitting to his left, but I did not see any other children there. All of a sudden, he sat facing forward, as if the teacher or some authority figure had just walked into the room. He saw me, because he looked my way and smiled.

After a while, Annette, Cathy, and I went with Florence Drake to see the upstairs. I saw the little boy at the dining room table there. He was looking very hungrily at the bowl of fake fruit. I told him that it was not real and not to try and eat it. I saw him again next to Cathy looking inside her jacket pocket on her right side. Then I went downstairs to join the other women who were there with us. The next time I saw the boy, he was in the little entryway, and his eyes were sunken in, and he was holding his stomach. I don't know if he was showing me what he looked like before he died. I just don't know.....but I did say I would accept whatever came through.

Annette also wrote about her perspective on what she picked up on that day:

I saw the ghost of a Spanish man who talked to me about how he hung around the Historical Society building because his wife and daughter were buried in the area, and so he felt that he had to protect their graves. He told me he lived during the 1700s, and talked a little of what his life was like there. He went on to explain to me that there was another building on the site of where the Historical building is now, where he lived ages ago. I could see him, and I described what he looked like, and later drew a sketch of him. He was a thin man, with a thin mustache, and was very good-looking, wearing a big Spanish hat.

When we all went upstairs with the curator of the museum, I saw a buggy, and asked the curator if it was a doctor's buggy. She said no, that it was the mailman's buggy back in the 1800s. I kept getting information from my spirit guides that a doctor had used it. A couple weeks later,

Florence produced a photo of a doctor using this buggy with his wife in front of their farmhouse back in the 1800s. Florence told me that now the society would have to change the history about the buggy.

*photograph courtesy of Annette Parlin*

*Chapter 27*

# Spirit Lady in Mount Vernon

I am Annette Parlin, and I am a medium-clairvoyant from Temple, Maine. A couple of years ago, I was down visiting a friend of mine on Ithiel Gordon Road in Mount Vernon, near Parker Pond. She was driving her horse, and we were riding in her buggy. It was a beautiful fall day, and I had my digital camera. I took pictures as we went along. There was no wind, just a perfectly beautiful fall day. I was just shooting and shooting, and we went down a few dirt roads.

When I went home, I downloaded my pictures on my computer. I looked at each one, and then I stopped and thought, "Whoa, what is this?!" I zoomed in on one of the photos I had taken, and there in the middle of road, it looks like someone dancing and twirling! So I blew the picture up some more, and it looks like a woman dancing in the middle of the road. When I have shown it to other people, they see it, too. So it's not like I tell them; I just ask them what they see. She's just twirling.

Now, I showed it to my skeptic friend Wanda who was there with me that day, and she said, "Oh it's just a dust wind."

I said, "Now wait a minute, there was no wind that day, and if you look at the horse's mane and tail they are not blowing in the wind. Nothing. It was dead still that day."

What's really interesting is that it looks like she has this white gown up close to her body, and on top of that it looks like she has a dress with a sheer material that you can see through. But you can't see through her, she is blocking the sunlight. It's like she's really there and she's solid. And she even creates a little shadow. So when she's twirling, the sheer is reflecting off the sunlight, and you can see the back of her hair, and it is like she is standing on her tippy toes. It is very beautiful!

I called her my spirit lady, but I didn't know who she was, and I didn't see her when it was happening, and the horse never saw it either. The horse was looking away, and he would have looked toward her if he had seen her. I remember the horse was fidgety that day, and he kept looking in the woods, but I didn't know the horse, so I didn't think much of it.

Someone had told me that Mount Vernon was a very spiritual town. I found out later that the spirit lady was actually my mother on the other side, and she was just happy to see me, and she was twirling in the middle of the road, and enjoying the day! I have captured billions of orbs, but I have never captured anything like this before.

*photograph courtesy of Annette Parlin*

*photograph courtesy of The Pelletier Family*

*Chapter 28*

# The Pelletier House in Fayette

*Richard and Becky Pelletier live in a very old house in Fayette. They are a well-known musical family who perform together with traditional gospel music. Their guitars, banjos, fiddles, mandolins, and lobos are beautifully handcrafted by Richard himself. Becky has deep roots in this town, as her family goes back several generations in the Moose Hill area. Children Julie, Lori, Rick, and the late Derrick, grew up in this historic home and experienced many spooky events. The Pelletier family shared many charming ghost stories of their home.*

Annette, her husband Ron, my friend Betsy, and I spent an afternoon with Richard "Dick" and Becky Pelletier, and their daughter, Lori, who were all wonderful story tellers.

Captain Richard Tilton built this house in 1785, and it had at one time been a tavern, according to Dick, who knows plenty about local history. Becky said that Tilton was buried in the cemetery down by the woods near the North Fayette Community Church. The house is also thought to have been connected to the Underground Railroad.

It is identified on the 1856 map of Fayette as having more than one occupant, one with the name "T. F. Palmer," and also "S. Walton's Hotel" and "P. O." In 1879, it was occupied by the family of "L. F. Bessey."

Annette immediately said, "They are making me smile, and I am getting a little girl, and she's African American. I'm not surprised," she said," because I thought I was getting something about the Underground Railroad activity in your house. That is such a rich history, and it left such an imprint here on this house."

Annette saw the spirit of a little girl peeking at her from around the big brick center fireplace in the kitchen, near where we were sitting around the kitchen table.

Becky said she was not surprised Annette saw someone in that area of the kitchen. "I had a friend visiting from New York and he was sitting across from us at this table, and he kept looking over his shoulder at the microwave, so much that I noticed it," she said. "Finally, when he realized we had something here in the house, it was almost like he went 'whew!' He said he could sense a child hiding behind this planter, and he was looking into the microwave trying to find the little child's reflection!"

Annette watched the little girl, and described her as appearing to be playing hide-and-seek, with her finger up to her lips and saying, "Shhh!"

Becky said, "We were, at one time, having weekly prayer meetings in the house, and there was a minister who was familiar with spirits. During a break in the prayer meeting, the subject of spirits came up, and Dick and I were looking at each other, because we had never said too much before to anyone, because they might think we were not quite right! We just kept looking at each other back and forth, and I said that we hear noises in this house, and the minister said, 'Do you want to take care of it once and for all?' And we said yes. So, he had everybody at the prayer meeting stand and hold hands and he just said this very simple prayer, asking the spirit to go to the place where God intended it to go."

Annette explained her knowledge about the spirit world:

A spirit can go anywhere it wants to, and the difference between a ghost and a spirit is that a ghost doesn't know that it's a ghost, and is earthbound. Something is keeping it here. Lots of times they just love the house or the farm, or they may not have believed in God or an afterlife when they were alive, so when they died, they just hung around, and didn't go anywhere. That's a ghost. A spirit is someone like you or I, who has died. We know that there is a God and an afterlife, so that's what we call the "other side," just to keep it simple. Call it heaven, or whatever you want, but I just call it the afterlife, and it is a place of beauty and light and love. Spirits can be anywhere they want to be. A spirit of someone you love who has passed is always around you. A spirit is energy; you can't kill it.

I'm getting that this little girl is not a ghost, she is a spirit. She just likes it here, and she comes and goes as she pleases. Because I am here, and we are all here talking about ghosts and spirits, they are interested and attracted to us. They come, and they feel the vibration and the energy, and so they just show up. They know what's going on here with us, and what we are doing.

You don't have to be afraid; they have a very good feeling. You have a very good house here. And so when someone wants a spirit to be gone, and they wish it away, the spirit or ghost complies, because they don't want to scare anyone. Sometimes, they just want us to know that they are around. So, you might feel the presence of a loved one who has passed away, or you might be suddenly thinking about them, and that's just their way of letting you know that they are around. You could think of them as being like air; they are not a body like us. They don't need bodies on the other side, but sometimes they show themselves to us in human form, so we would recognize them, like when I can see the little girl over there by the chimney. So, you don't have to be afraid of things that you hear and see around your home. You have a lovely home and it has a very good feeling.

"So," said Becky, "you are like the lady on the Ghost Whisperer television show."

Annette, laughing, said, "Oh that's just Hollywood! But, yes, I can hear and see spirits and ghosts, and I can also pick up on their feelings. Sometimes they allow me to know how they're feeling, so that helps me communicate with them. I am a medium clairvoyant, and it is a gift. We all are spiritual, and we all have the gift, but most people have lost touch with it. When you hear of this type of gift running in families, it's because it is talked about and believed, and encouraged. I feel I am just a messenger, and I relate what I hear and see, that's all. It's all very normal actually, it's just that many people have lost this, but we all have intuition."

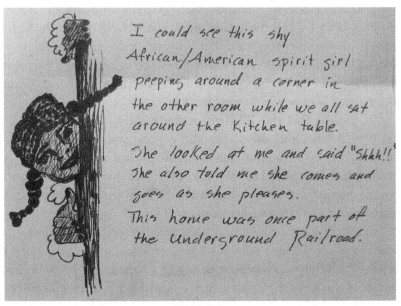

*drawing by Annette Parlin*

Becky continued with her stories:

The first night we were here, in October of 1964, we set up our bedrooms and went to bed about nine o'clock. We hadn't even gone to sleep yet when we heard a noise down in the kitchen, like pots and pans falling, and a big crashing sound! It really sounded like all the cupboards came open and all the dishes just came crashing out on the floor. So we went downstairs, and nothing was out of place. Everything was in perfect order. We went all over the house and we couldn't find anything. So, we just went back to bed.

At that time my husband worked from 11 p.m. to 7 a.m. I woke up about 4:30 a.m., and it sounded like somebody was hammering on the woodstove down in the kitchen. I was so scared I didn't even get out of bed. (She laughs.) It was very loud; it was just pound, pound, pound! Well, I used to sing with this woman whose grandparents used to live in this house. Probably it was in the 1920s or 1930s that they lived here. One night when we were at chorus practice, Elaine mentioned to me about how noisy this house was. I didn't pick up on it at first. Now, this house is put together with pegs, and so when it's very windy outside this house is very creaky, and so I thought that was what she meant.

A few years later, I said, "Elaine did you ever hear noises in this house?" She said that yes, she had tried to tell me one time. I told her that I had heard someone banging on the woodstove, and it sounded like a hammer.

"Yes, we used to hear that."

"I also have heard a body falling down the stairs."

She looked at me and said, "Yes! We used to hear that, too, out on the back stairway!"

Now, we have four flights of stairs in this old house, and she didn't hesitate, she said, "In those little back stairs." That's exactly where I heard it!

It was six o'clock in the morning, and there is no way that I was drowsy at that time. I was putting up the kid's lunches, and it sounded like one of the kids had fallen down the stairs. I dropped the sandwiches and ran, and there was no one there at all.

At this moment in the conversation, Annette spoke up and said she was getting that there was a tall, thin man. "I think he was elderly, and he slipped and fell down the stairs."

Dick laughed and said, "A lot of people have fallen down those stairs, including me!"

Lori spoke:

I was in the guest bedroom, which once was the office, and I was sleeping in the brass bed. All of a sudden in the middle of the night, I woke right up and I could hear footsteps coming. They were so gentle and soft, but I could hear them coming. They went around the bed, and then they went around the bed again. They walked out the door halfway down those stairs, only halfway down. I looked around, and I just lay there listening. I was maybe twelve or thirteen years old.

One time I was sitting here drawing for an art class, and my parents were at work. I was an adult then. I was working on my project, and I could hear a sound coming from my parents' bedroom, like a heavy man with big footsteps. Now, it was windy out, but I just stopped drawing and listened, and I could hear him just walking around up there. Well, I just walked right out the door and went over to the neighbor's house, with the pencil still in my hand. The neighbor came back over with me to get my stuff, and when we walked in, it sounded like a whole woodpile in the cellar had tumbled down. My friend just looked at me and said, "Let's get out of here!" Now, the footsteps of this man were not like the tiny footsteps I had heard in my bedroom that night. These were footsteps of a big man, and a heavy person.

Becky spoke up now, and said, "We used to hear that sound of the woodpile falling, probably six or seven times, and it seemed like it made the whole house shake."

Dick had another story: Now here's the other part about the woodpile, and I told you that you just would not believe this story! Because every time someone would come here, and I would tell the story, I know they were thinking that this was just nonsense. Well, we had a man and his wife stay here one weekend, and I was showing him around, and we went downstairs, and I showed him the woodpile and everything. Our woodpile is attached to the back of the house, and we can get to it by way of the cellar, as that's where our wood furnace is.

He said, "Well, yeah, that looks nice."

Now, I had all the wood piled on one side of the woodshed. The shed was not part of this house; I built it myself. It's attached to the house. We came back upstairs, and I was telling him all these stories. All of a sudden, you could hear that woodpile shake, and it shook the whole side of the house! We went back down cellar and I opened that door, and that woodpile was on the other side of the wall, all piled up. Well, to this day, I don't know how that happened!

Becky said, "Tell them the Kendall Morse story." Kendall is in the Hall of Fame, and was just recommended for a Grammy. He was a folk artist from Maine. He was a wonderful singer, until he got cancer in his throat, and couldn't sing anymore.

Dick went on: He was up here visiting, and my garage used to be a summer kitchen. I don't know what we were doing, but I was sitting at the workbench out there, and I was telling him stories. Again, here's another example where I'm telling somebody a story, and they don't believe what I'm saying.

Kendall said, "Oh, I don't believe in that stuff, there's always an explanation for things like that." All of a sudden, over in the corner, it sounded like something hit the floor, and he looked over that way. Then, what looked like a coin started rolling, and it rolled across the floor right up to him. Right in front of him, it made a turn and started spinning around and around and around, right in front of him, and then it stopped! It was a large penny, I have it right over there in the cupboard, and the date on it is 1885. Well, Kendall bent over and picked it up, and said "Wow!" It made a believer out of him right that very minute.

Annette said her spirit guides were telling her that it was a man who sent that coin rolling to Dick's friend, as if to say to him, "Now you will believe! Things do happen here!"

Becky went over to the cupboard and found the coin, and Annette picked it up and held it in her hand. She said she felt a tremendous sadness when she touched it. She said she felt it belonged to a man who had died a very tragic death. Annette said that the man who sent the coin rolling was indeed a ghost.

Lori wondered if this could be the ghost of a boy that she said she had met when she was a child. She said he was watching her when she was playing in her playhouse one day:

Our neighbors Carl and Alice let me have a playhouse in the attic of the ell that was attached to the house. I spent many hours playing there. A day or so before, everything in the playhouse had gotten moved around somehow. I accused my sister of doing it, but she said no. The ghost of the boy that I saw was sitting with his hands wrapped around his knees, and I couldn't really tell if he was a boy or girl, at the time. He had tan-colored clothes on, all raggedy, and I remember he had black hair and dark eyes. He just stared at me; he was all crunched up on the floor in the corner, watching me.

Annette said, "He comes from over there," pointing across the road to another house.

Lori asked, "Is the ghost's name George?"

Lori explained that she had looked in the history books a few years ago, trying to figure out who the ghost from her childhood might have been. "I'm so sorry that I didn't try to speak to him then." Lori said she wished she had tried to play with him, and that she felt sorry for him now.

Annette said he probably did relate to her because she was then a child herself.

"He's an old ghost," Annette said.

Lori said she had read that there was a little boy of about eight years old who had lived at the house across the street, and that he had died somehow.

Annette asked if there was a stream nearby, and said she felt that the little boy played there with his sister a lot. Annette said that the boy's sister was with him now, and confirmed that she was a couple years older than he, and matched the information Lori said she had read about when she did research.

"His name was George Palmer," Lori said.

Becky told us that there was an elderly couple who lived across the street when they first moved into this house. "They were like grandparents to us," Becky said. "And they let Lori have a playhouse when she was little. It was in their shed, and it was all fixed up."

"Did you ever see other ghosts?" Annette asked.

"No," Lori answered, "not in that house. But now I know I am not crazy!" Lori laughed, as Annette had validated Lori's childhood ghost encounters.

Lori said that she had seen a ghost, just a couple of years before, at her neighbor's house up on the hill where a log cabin stands. Lori described her as a woman who was tall and had Indian features. She said she wrote down everything she saw that day to document it.

"For some reason, I knew her name was Martha. When I asked her what her name was, she didn't answer, and I said, 'Well I have to go.' Right then, her name came to me, 'Martha!' I just knew that was her name."

When asked how this ghost was dressed, Lori answered, "Just the same as the little boy, with tan or gold-colored raggedy clothes made of a canvas-like material. It was a plain dress, and I saw her whole body, and even her very masculine-looking hands."

Annette said the ghost woman was appearing to her now, and was pointing in the direction of the log cabin up the road. The ghost woman was indicating that her house was somewhere up behind the log cabin, when she was living. It was a little house, and she stressed "little" house, down over the hill. Lori said that there were cellar holes up in that direction. Lori asked Annette, why the ghost appeared to her.

Annette said that the ghost may have liked Lori's energy, and her openness, "And she just liked you."

Lori also commented that the ghost woman gave her a stern look. Annette said the ghost corrected her, and said that's just the way she looked. The ghost indicated through Annette that life was very hard back then, hence the serious expression.

Annette said the ghost woman told her, "I was not a pretty woman, but I worked hard."

Lori repeated, "I was not crazy then, I really did see that ghost!"

Annette reassured Lori that she was indeed very intuitive, and that the spirits or ghosts come to her because she is very open-minded.

"It's like they say, 'Oh, she is open and she's willing to see me. I think I will show myself to her and talk to her!'"

Lori admitted that she can tell when someone is going to die, and she related a couple of intriguing but personal stories about when this had happened to her.

Dick spoke up and told a story about a time when his oldest daughter Julie was baby-sitting, and he and Becky had to come home early that night.

"The kids were scared to death because a rocking chair in the other room would not stop rocking. It had gotten to the point where it was almost as if the rocking chair was going to tip over, it was rocking so much!"

Becky continued, "Julie was on the phone, and she was out in the hall hanging the phone up, and she looked into the living room, and the rocking chair was tipped right back almost on the back tip of the rockers, it was tipped back so far! She was scared to death!"

Annette said that there was a little girl, a ghost, and that she was not trying to scare them, but just trying to get their attention. "She wasn't really in the chair, but was standing beside it, tipping it back on the tips of the rocker, really trying to get your attention."

Lori recalled the time when her brother was sitting in a swivel rocker watching television and her mother was sitting on the couch reading. There was a guitar leaning against a beam by the piano. Lori was in the kitchen doing the supper dishes. All of a sudden, the guitar went plink, plink as though someone had plucked the strings.

Derrick, her brother, swiveled around in the rocker and looked at his mother and asked, "Who did that?"

Becky thought he was teasing her, and said, "You did!"

Lori heard their conversation, and came into the living room just in time to hear the guitar go plink, plink again while Derrick was still looking at his mother. He exclaimed, "I'm getting out of here," and rushed out of the room.

Dick said there could be an explanation for that kind of thing, as he builds instruments and said that it is possible, if you put a guitar over by a cold wall, that the strings could tighten up and make a sound on their own.

Becky insisted, "That wasn't it, I saw it move and make a sound on its own!"

Becky said that over the years, they have had many house guests stay who have experienced many spooky things and heard footsteps, and so on. Her granddaughter, Serenity, once stayed with them, and had heard footsteps around her bed during the night.

There was another time when Richard and Becky were away at a bluegrass festival, and a relative had stayed at their house. "They came in, and after they had gone to bed, they heard a sound like a bowling ball up in the attic, and it rolled from one end of the attic to the other. Well, if you have ever seen that attic, you would know that the attic is too cluttered for a ball to roll from one end to the other!" Becky said that she later heard that the sound of a rolling ball is something that many people have experienced when they have heard haunting noises in their houses.

Dick said, "It is all quiet around here now; we don't hear things anymore," indicating that the Pastor's blessing had cured them of the ghosts in their house.

Annette laughed, and said, "Oh, yes, they are still around here! But they may be just respecting your wishes, if you had asked them not to disturb you anymore. This house is loaded," and she laughed again!

Everyone laughed as Dick said, "Well, we put on a good show for them!"

Dick said that his mother had died from cancer many years ago at

age fifty-four, and had visited in Becky's and Lori's dreams one night. Becky continued with the story, describing a night two years after her mother-in-law's death.

"I dreamed that I could hear voices coming from Lori's room. So in my dream, I got up and went in to Lori's room. I looked, and his mother was lying beside Lori in her bed, and they were talking. Oh it's just Grammy talking to Lori, I thought, even though in my dream I knew that she was dead. I just went back to bed. In the morning, lo and behold, Lori got up and said, 'Grammy came to visit me last night!'"

Lori says that even now when she wakes up early in the mornings she sometimes knows that her grandmother has been there with her.

Annette stated that she believed that in our dreams we can actually go into another state or realm where our spirit can actually be with our loved ones who have passed on. "We are merely energy, and our soul or spirit, or whatever you want to call it, is able to travel and go wherever it wants. That's how our loved ones can come in and comfort us and talk to us in our dream state, when we are not scared of them. So, for example, your grandmother didn't want to scare you, so she came into your dream to visit you."

Becky said, "There was another time after my father had died, and I was lying in bed and thinking about him. I felt a cool touch on my cheek. I knew it was him."

Annette said that was "Love coming through from the other side."

Annette said, "I'm getting that you're experiencing a lot of generational goings-on here. You've got the Underground Railroad and the pre-railroad, the spirits are telling me, and now, there is a Civil War soldier over there in the corner." Annette explained the home's rich history may be why the house has always been so active.

Becky told us another story about a friend of hers named Lois, who came to visit one day with her husband and their kids. "They were sitting in the living room, and the kids were outdoors. Her husband was sitting on the piano bench for a while; then all of a sudden, I noticed that he went outside, and I thought maybe he was getting bored with us talking or something. Later, I looked up, and he was out sitting in the car." She laughed. "I thought he had gone out to watch the kids!" More laughter. "Afterward, he told Lois that he had seen a 'mist' in the mirror above the couch, and he was so scared he had to leave!"

Becky said she has never seen a "mist" or anything physical here, for that matter. "Oh, I've heard plenty, but I have never seen anything."

"The only thing I've ever seen," said Dick, "was when the woodpile moved."

Lori talked about a gravestone marker with the initials "BMP" that she found under the steps across the road. Annette asked her why there would be a gravestone underneath the doorstep, and Lori said, "The neighbor's house used to be a casket factory."

She explained that when the people who lived there before were leveling the front steps, they found some gravestones buried under the steps.

After a tour of this lovely old home, we ended our visit with many thanks to the Pelletiers for their great stories and warm hospitality. It was a very memorable afternoon!

Chapter 29

# Leon Robert's Reincarnation Story

My name is Leon Chester Roberts, and I grew up in Winthrop. I am a licensed funeral practitioner, which is a fancy way of saying a mortician or an undertaker. I am a sixth-generation undertaker, and I am named after my great-grandfather Leon Roberts. His grandfather started a funeral home in Wayne. Then they moved to Readfield and got burned down, and then my great-grandfather moved to Winthrop. I lived in Chicago for about twelve years after I graduated from college. I moved back to Winthrop in 1994.

About two years ago, a friend of mine from Chicago who had been working on the Oprah Winfrey Show came here to visit with me for a couple of weeks. In September that year, she called me and said that they were doing this show on Oprah for the Great American Smokeout. They were trying to get as many people as possible in the country to quit smoking. She had about eight women and two or three men who were going to be on her show, and some of them were backing out three days before the show was going to be aired. My friend asked me to be on the show. She told me I had one day to decide. She said, "You need to have someone videotape you smoking for a couple of days." So I did that, and then I sent them the tape.

They called me and said, "Can we fly you out here tomorrow?" So they flew me out there, and lo and behold, I was the only man on the show! There were eight women and myself. We were given the tools to quit smoking, and some of us quit the day of the show.

I did quit smoking, and it had been about two weeks since I had smoked. They asked me back on the Oprah show for a variety-type show. Part of the variety show was to check on the people who had quit smoking. I was actually the only one who had quit. There were two other women who had stopped smoking for a couple of days, and they wanted their impressions. They asked me how I was doing, and I said I felt great; I thought I was over the smoking thing pretty much.

I came home, and about a month later I got a call, and they said that Oprah had come out of a meeting, and said, "I want to see if I can get Leon to come back on for the show that we're going to be doing." It was a show on past life regression, featuring Dr. Brian Weiss, who is a well-known psychiatrist in this country who specializes in hypnotherapy. He had been on the show about twenty years before, and people then thought of it as kind of a joke, and weren't really accepting of that kind of thing. This time he was on he had a much bigger following. For example, they did a survey and found that about sixty percent of the population believes in reincarnation or similar theories.

They called me and asked me if I would like to come back. They said that Oprah was interested in learning what was going on inside of my head. Because I'm a funeral director, and I had been on her show a couple of times, she wanted to know if I would be willing to be hypnotized and to learn if I had anything interesting going on in my past.

Before I agreed to do this, I read Dr. Weiss's book, *Many Lives, Many Masters*. Before I got through the first twenty pages, I called them up and said, "Yeah, I'll do it." I was really hesitant afterwards, because I didn't think I would have anything interesting to offer. I have seen people hypnotized in comedy clubs, but I always questioned whether I could be hypnotized or not. I didn't know if my mind could be relaxed like that long enough to be hypnotized. So I said I might be wasting their time, but I would come out. They said that if nothing happens then nothing happens, and we won't worry about it.

There were about five or six of us who had been hypnotized on past shows. Everybody kept going in with Dr. Weiss, and coming out about every twenty-five minutes. They would come out and be thinking about what happened, and most of them would say it was a pretty good experience.

It took me about twenty minutes to be hypnotized, and they mock his office from Miami, and I just sat in there, and there were cameras all around but I couldn't see them. I didn't think I could be hypnotized; that was my number-one worry. I was kind of warm to this past life idea and listening to others' stories and what they went through was kind of interesting. I still didn't think it would be successful.

I went in, and the hypnosis was completely different than I thought it was going to be. Dr. Weiss explained that it was a very deep meditative state. He would get you in a very relaxed and comfortable state. So anyway, the first thing he did was to have me go back into my childhood. I didn't know this until later, but it took me about twenty minutes, and eventually I was hypnotized. I don't know how these thoughts came to me or anything, but he had me go back to my childhood to a happy memory, and I remember my father being very supportive of me. He wanted me to do something, but he wouldn't push me into it; he was very supportive of me. I remembered a few incidents playing basketball in junior high. These things that I could recall, I could remember them like it was right now. They weren't things that I could remember normally if I was just talking to you.

Then, he had me go further back, even back to when I was born. I remembered coming home from the hospital, and my sister was coming up to me, and she was all excited. I remember people were all around me, and I felt very loved. Then he asked me to go back to when I was inside my mother's womb. I didn't think I could go back to that time, but I was in this very, very deep state then. He said that only about twenty percent of people can be induced to go that deeply into hypnosis, and he said I did that pretty easily.

This is when it got kind of weird, when he asked me to go back to see if there was another life. I started recalling another life. I was near the end of this other life. I was in a plane during a war, and I was sitting in back; I was a gunner. I was firing, and it was all cloudy. I could remember all that I was telling him; people were firing at me, trying to hit our plane. I was firing back, and I remembered I stopped firing because I didn't know who to fire at. I didn't know who was us and who was them! Then we got shot down, because I wasn't shooting back. I wasn't firing my rifles, or my guns. It was the end of my life, and I was scared. I was just scared to death. I was just outside of myself.

Then once I died, Dr. Weiss asked me how I felt. I said I was very relieved. He asked me if I had learned anything in that life. I told him I had learned to trust my instincts, and to not do something that I didn't want to do, and that I didn't feel bad about that, or regret what I had done. There's a lot more to it, but it has been a while.

I interjected at this point and told Leon that I remembered that when I had seen the videotape of the show, Dr. Weiss had said that Leon was an advanced spirit or soul, and that is why he was reluctant to kill another human being. I also remembered when I saw the videotape that Leon was in anguish over his guilty feeling that he had caused his co-pilot and himself to die.

He took me back into another life, and in this one, too, I was coming to the end of a life. I was witnessing someone being raped and beaten. It's really weird, because when I think about this now, when I woke up, I was just exhausted. I did a lot of crying and sobbing, because I was at the end of each life, and it was ending. After each life, I would experience this feeling like I was just floating. I have read some books about this, and it's really interesting, because part of this theory is that energy goes on and it never really stops. You learn that when you are alive, energy just changes form. After you die, your spirit or soul, or whatever you want to call it, just kind of hovers for a while until it goes into another body. It's weird to think of it this way.

I guess I have been open to this type of thing before, but when I decided to go on the show I was really thinking of it as getting a free vacation, or as if it was kind of a joke. Also, I thought it would be interesting to hear other people's stories. What happened to me was beyond what I would have imagined. You know, I wouldn't be able to act like that if I tried. I just couldn't make up stuff like that. I don't know where it came from. Sometimes I don't believe it one hundred percent, but there is something to it. There is really something after this life.

Now that I have been on the Oprah show and have gone through this, I think of life in a completely different way. Now that I have gone through this, I know that life isn't just this. I completely believe that there is more, and that we go on. It's a relief to know I don't need to worry about dying. Working in the funeral business, where I have to think about death every day, I feel like this just isn't all there is. I know there is more.

My grandmother died last summer, and I was really having a hard time with it, even though she was ninety-four. Because of this experience, I believe it's just a relief for her, and I know that her spirit goes on. It makes you think that when someone you love dies, this is not the end, and that you will see them again. It just makes this life that much better, because you are not worried about the end of it. You are not scared of death. I don't want to die tomorrow, but I'm not afraid of death at all. That's how I think of it now.

Another thing I noticed when I came out of hypnosis: I was cold and shivering. When I woke up, it was just like, "Wow!" I could remember everything that had been said, but I wondered, where did this stuff come from and what just happened?

Dr. Weiss asked me how long I thought I had been under. I thought that it had been maybe twenty minutes, and I was shocked when he told me that it had been about two hours! He said that when people go into a deep meditative state, that often their body temperature lowers slightly. These are the kind of things that really make me believe.

Here's another thing. When I sleep, I really snore, but I wasn't snoring, and I wasn't dreaming; it was deep hypnosis. It was really unbelievable; everyone should experience it.

It's more difficult to explain the second hypnosis experience. I was at the end of that life, too, and was witnessing the rape and beating of a woman. I just sat there and watched, frozen in fear. It was like a bad dream where you can't react, and I was afraid. The next thing I remember, I was grabbed by the throat and I got hit on the head, and just blacked out. When I came to, I was in a dark place, just laid out. Then something was sitting on top of me and crushing me, and I died. I just felt so guilty that I didn't do anything about it (the rape). When I died, I just felt so relieved, and then I realized that there wasn't anything I could do about it. So I was more at peace about it after I died.

Dr. Weiss asked me who the female being raped was. I hesitated and hesitated, and I didn't want to say it. He said to me, "It's okay, just say it," and then I just blurted out that it was my sister! She wasn't my sister in that life, though. I've been reading about this in books because I think about it a lot. I've been feeling like I need to get a sense of what happened to me.

It's not all black-and-white, but what they say is that people tend to migrate in groups to another life. Someone that you are close to in this life could be with you in another life, but they may be your enemy in that next life. For example, your ex-husband in this life could be your nasty neighbor in your next life. Your mother in this life could be your sister in your past life. It's a lot to believe in, but it's something that I think about a lot. I was really upset that I let this girl die, and that I didn't do anything about it. When Dr. Weiss asked me about this girl, I told him I didn't know her at all in that life, but I knew that she was my sister Lynn in this life.

Lynn and I don't really get along that well. Yes, we work together, but we are really very opposite people in many ways. My issue with her is that she is the type of person who is busy all the time, and I worry that she's just going to melt down someday. She goes and goes and goes and goes. I worry about her, and sometimes get angry at her because she never stops. I'm just the opposite—I try to enjoy life. Most of the time I'm just smelling the roses! With the two of us being that different, I guess we frustrate each other. If it wasn't for the business, we probably would get along better.

Dr. Weiss's explanation is that I am protective of her now because I feel so bad that I didn't protect her in the past life. We had a great time when Lynn came out with me for the taping of the show, along with our sister Val. We had never all gone on vacation together, so we had a great bonding experience. My sister Lynn was hypnotized also, though it had nothing to do with me. She had some interesting past life regressions, too, that made sense to her life and helped her out. We both unloaded a lot of stuff, and we seemed to accept each other better after that. We still have some difficulties, but nothing like before. It's really like night and day for me. I can accept that it is her life and that she should live it the way she is supposed to.

I have also read that when you have gone through a past life regression and worked out issues from a past life, it can help you with any fears or phobias that you have in this life. If, for example, you have a fear of someone putting their hands around your throat, or of falling through the ice, and so on, it may be because of an event or trauma from one of your past lives. So if you can work it out under hypnosis, you can improve your experience in this life. It really helps you work through those issues. More and more, this experience has definitely left me a believer in something. And I want to learn more.

This is another experience that I had after the hypnosis experience and past life regression, which involved being in an airplane. Months later I visited an Air Force Base in Tucson, Arizona with my girlfriend and her parents, who live in Phoenix. Her father works for General Electric, which makes the engines for these planes. He wanted to show me the Base. We drove down to Tucson and went to visit the Air Force Base.

I wasn't that excited about going, but I went because he wanted me to go see the Base. My girlfriend's mother said to me, "It's really important to him, so just pretend that you like it."

We arrived and immediately, I felt chills all over, like a kid in a candy store! I was looking around and really overwhelmed by the feelings that I was experiencing. We went all around, and he showed me these different hangars. Then we went to a boneyard where there are about forty-five hundred different aircraft parked in the desert. They were all World War II and post-World War II era aircraft. It was so interesting. We went over to this airplane, and it had this gunner bay down underneath. When I saw that, I nearly started to cry. I didn't want my girlfriend or her parents to see me like that, so I walked over to this other aircraft. I thought, "Wow, this is so amazing." I got up into it, and I said, "Oh that must be where the guy crawls down into it."

Then the guy working there said, "Yeah, that's right." We went down by the tail, and there was this bubble where you sit underneath the plane with the guns. You kind of get flipped into it, and then it goes down where you sit.

My girlfriend's father sat down and he said, "I think it works this way."

I said, "No, I think it works this way." I told him how I thought it worked.

He said, "No, I don't think so."

I said, "Let's ask this guide." It turns out the guide we talked to was in World War II, and this was the plane that he flew in. We asked him how it worked. He showed us how the guy would get in up top and go down through to the bottom. It turned out I was right! I looked over at my girlfriend's father, and he had this weird look on his face as if he couldn't figure out how I knew that.

He said, "How the heck did you know that?"

"I don't know," I said, and then I just had shivers all over. It was really weird.

I thought about my experience under hypnosis, and I thought, "Am I really feeling something from another life?" So I proceeded to stay in this place for about five hours that day, and finally everybody was saying it's time to go.

My girlfriend's father came over to me and said, "Come on Leon, I know you're really enjoying this, but we can come back next year. The girls really want to get out of here!"

Then my girlfriend's mother came up to me and said, "You know, you can knock it off a little bit; you're coming on too strong!"

For months after the experience on the Oprah show on Past Life Regression, I tried to figure out what happened to me that day. I can't explain certain things that happened. I think about it, and try to process it all the time.

I didn't have the flying dreams again for about a year and a half after, but the last few months I've been having them again. I have had a recurring dream all my life where I am flying, and someone is chasing me and trying to kill me. I was always just barely getting away from them. The flying dreams I have now are pleasurable and nice. I dream that I'm flying, and it's wonderful, and when I remember these dreams I just want to go back and dream them again.

It's a funny thing, but about three or four years ago I saw Evelyn Potter, who is a spiritual reader, and she told me that I had astral-traveled in my dreams. It's really strange, but she said that I actually came into her house one time and I was watching TV in her living room. She said that I came to visit her! She told me that I actually travel all over the place at night. In the mornings, I am always so tired because I have been so active during the night. This is what she told me. It's weird, because I do have these dreams where I am flying. I fly over to people's houses and into their houses, I fly down over the lake, and things like that; it's weird. I do this almost every night. It's awesome! It's so real, I will be flying down over Maranacook Lake and I am flying just over the water!

I remembered when I watched the videotape of the Oprah show that Leon had talked about having a message to share, and I thought it was awesome.

He went on: Yeah, that's right; I have always thought that being a funeral director had to be a calling. I went to school in Arizona, and then I started out being a bond trader in Chicago. It was high-stress, but then I moved back to Maine, and I feel like that's the way it was supposed to be. I feel comfortable around death, and dead people. You know, I can't really explain this, but I feel energy when I am around them. On the show, Dr. Weiss asked me under hypnosis if the dead people talked to me. I said they don't talk to me, I don't hear any voices or anything like that, but it's energy, it's just a feeling I get. It's really weird and hard to explain. It's almost like I'm talking to people out loud.

I feel like it's my job to comfort people, and that they want me to tell their loved ones that they are okay and that they are okay where they are. I can help people because of my experience, and it helps me in my work. I believe in what I'm doing, and I believe in the crossover. This life is not all there is. I feel like if I won the lottery, I would still do this job because I love it. I'm supposed to be doing this; there is no doubt in my mind.

After the show and the experience with hypnotism, everything in my life changed. Now I just feel at peace with my life.

*Chapter 30*

# LeeAnn's Ghost Stories

*LeeAnn was a classmate of mine from Winthrop. She told me she has had many experiences with ghosts all her life, in every house she has lived in. Here are some of her stories:*

I will go back to the mid- to late 1970s, to my childhood home on Stanley Road in East Winthrop. I was a teenager, and my stuff always seemed to go missing. I just figured that I lost it or someone put it somewhere, considering that I lived with my father and brothers, and we weren't the most organized bunch. We had one housekeeper that wouldn't clean there alone because she was scared. She felt as if someone else was in the house with her, and she said it scared her half to death!

Sometimes lights would go on and off by themselves. After careful inspection of the lights we never found them faulty. I never thought much of it; it was just strange. I had friends who were definitely creeped out by that house. I honestly never felt that way myself.

There was one particular night I have never forgotten. We were watching movies—my brother and his girlfriend, myself, and a few others. I slipped on my sister-in-law's blue clogs and went to the store. I came home from the store and kicked them off in the kitchen by the door, right where they had been previously. A few hours later, she came out to the kitchen to leave, and she couldn't find her shoes, so we searched high and low, and couldn't find them. No one had come in the house and no one had left since I returned from the store. So I gave her a pair of my shoes with promises of locating hers the next day.

The next day I turned the place upside down, looked in all the closets, in all the rooms, under the furniture, under the baseboards, everywhere, and turned up no shoes! Years went by without them turning up, and finally they were forgotten. One day years later, I was looking for something, and I opened the coat closet by the front door, and there sat the blue pair of clogs sitting neatly on top of some other things. I was baffled at whose shoes they were as I stood looking down at them. A few minutes went by before it dawned on me! "OMG," I thought, "these can't be those long-forgotten clogs of my sister-in-law's, could they?" I jumped in my car and drove over to her house, showed her the shoes, and asked, "Are these the clogs that went missing years ago?"

She said, "Yes, where did you find them?"

I had looked in that same closet hundreds of times since those shoes went missing, and they were never there. I asked everyone if they had put them there, and no one had. It certainly was strange.

I had a favorite sweater that I never left anywhere which disappeared there, and again I looked everywhere. When I finally found it years later, it was just inside the attic door, folded up messily and set on a box. I had been in and out of the attic a few times a year since I lost it, but it wasn't there.

I always thought that we had a young girl ghost in that house, but I didn't ever see her. I don't know why I thought that; I just did.

Our family camp was on Cobbossee Lake, a great big place built by Governor Hill right around the turn of the century. We've all heard the footsteps walking in the hall upstairs; they scared my husband right out of the place! He thought it was my father, but my father was in town. He was alone with the footsteps.

One morning I was there with my one-year-old son. We had walked over from the camp next door where we were staying, and I was drinking my coffee in the kitchen when I heard someone walking upstairs. I thought it was my father's wife although her car wasn't there. As time went by, it became clear that no one was home but my son and me, and of course.......the footsteps.

If there are ghosts here, they seem to come and go. One time my father was at the refrigerator, and when he backed away from it, he ran into something. He said it felt like he was backing up into foam rubber. He turned to see what was there, and there was nothing.

The house my family and I live in now, built circa 1880s, sits just off the river. The original owner was an ice worker on the river. This house has never really alarmed or scared anyone. Some strange things have gone on, though. I'll start back when my seventeen-year-old daughter was small, and she always complained about things running around her bed at night. She came in and slept with us a lot. I always figured it was just her young imagination at work.

One night I heard an echoing "Hellooooo," as if someone was at the door hollering for us, but there was no one there. I figured it was just my imagination.

Another time, I was standing in the kitchen and my dog, Sadie, who is scared of nothing, as she is an aggressive big German shepherd, started barking this strange bark and looking at the air in front of me, but up higher. She was barking and barking, hair standing up all down her back, with her tail tucked between her legs. I had never seen her tail between her legs, ever! She was scared as she stood in the door, but wouldn't come into the kitchen, no matter what I did. It took me an hour before I could get her to come through the kitchen. I didn't see anything at all, but she sure seemed to.

My daughter sees the head and shoulders of what she says is the shadow of a man, upstairs outside her room quite often. My son's and daughter's rooms have a door that connects them, and it is always shut. Recently, the door started to shake back and forth violently, and it woke them both. They both went for the door at the same time, wondering what the other was doing. That has happened twice, and there is no breeze or anything to make it move like that. Really weird.

Many, many, many times I have heard things moving around

upstairs when no one is up there. I've never actually seen a ghost, but I have certainly experienced the presence of ghosts!

*photograph courtesy of Joan Stiehler*

*Chapter 31*

# Joan Stiehler's House in Wayne

*Joan Stiehler is a former Wayne resident who is a wonderful storyteller and a woman of many skills and talents, including home renovations, and has knowledge of local history. She lived in an old Cape Cod-style house in Wayne in the 1970s. She has a story to tell:*

I bought the house in the early 1970s, and it was in its semi-original condition at the time, I would say. It had asbestos siding on it, and vintage 1940s windows. It had the old horsehair plaster, and beautiful white pine floors. One of the reasons I was attracted to this property was because it was small. I wanted to do a restoration, and I felt that I could manage this house. There was another house at the same time for sale in Wayne, but I decided that house was just too big a project for me to undertake. I decided to purchase this property from an elderly man who was in his eighties. His name was Tom. He had bought it during World War II. Tom wanted to move closer to medical facilities and shopping areas, so he bought a piece of property down in Greene. We moved into this house.

Around 1980, we started to work on the house. The house was built around 1790. I was told by people who had lived in Wayne back in the 1940s, '30s, or '20s, long before my time, that there was a man who had lived in the house and had died there. It was wintertime, and he probably used wood for heat, no doubt. The story is his body was left there for a few days because his dog was vicious toward everybody. The dog was lying with his master, and wouldn't allow anyone to get close to the bed and touch the body. Well, they had to get a veterinarian, and I was told that he came from Winthrop. He had come out to Wayne by horse and wagon, so it had to have been very early on. It was mud season, and so he couldn't get through Wayne during that time. He had to cross down by Berry Pond to lead the horses through the mud, so I was told. He had to come out to Wayne to tranquilize the dog so that they could remove the body. The blessing was that it was cold, so that the body did not deteriorate, and the man was ultimately removed from the house.

Well, when this strange phenomenon seemed to happen over and over again, I began to wonder if maybe it was the man who had died in this house, and thought that maybe he hadn't left yet and his spirit was still here.

This is what happened. I thought I was imagining things at first. But our dog was aware of the presence of this spirit, and you would hear it walking across the floors upstairs. Sometimes you would hear the shutters rattle on the house, but I didn't have any shutters. And there was no wind, but you would hear the clattering of shutters upstairs! I said to myself, there are no shutters, what could that noise be? But always when the spirit would make itself known, our dog would start growling. She would look up at the ceiling, or the walls, or just look up in the air, and she would growl and growl. I began to realize that it wasn't just me hearing things, and I wasn't just imaging these things. It was really happening! I had never lived in a house before where I could feel a presence, other than the presence of living people, but never any spiritual presence that I was aware of.

One time I was in the kitchen, which was in the ell of the house, and I was reading a book. I was actually reading *The Thornbirds* at the time. I had the woodstove going so that it would heat the whole house, and the woodstove was in the kitchen. It was wintertime, and all of the windows of the house were closed; no doors were open.

Suddenly, the door from the kitchen, which led to the living room part of the house, flew shut! I got up and opened the door, and went back to reading at the kitchen table. The door shut again. I thought, this is so strange; there is no wind, and the dog is lying down on the floor over there. How did the door close the second time? So I got up again and opened the door, because if the door is closed, none of the heat could go to any of the other parts of the house. The third time the door closed, it was slammed! Bang! I thought, "Oh, the presence of the spirit is here again, and that must be who is closing this door!" I got up and once again opened the door. I was all alone in the house, or else I probably wouldn't have done this, but I had a conversation with the spirit. Because if anyone had heard me they would've thought I was crazy; they would call the people from AMHI to come and collect me!

I had a conversation with this spirit, and I spoke to the spirit telling it that I needed the door to be open so that it would heat the other parts of the house.

"Maybe at one time you lived in this house and there was no kitchen in the ell; that is possible," I said. "Maybe there was no ell. But now there is, and that is where all the heat is coming from. So I am going to ask you to be kind and please leave the door open. Please don't shut it again."

It didn't shut again. I couldn't believe it; I was holding a conversation with a spirit that I couldn't see or touch, that I didn't even know anything about, except for the occurrences that were happening. But repeatedly, I would hear this spirit opening doors and closing doors, walking upstairs in other parts of the house. I would go into the barn, where the steps would go up, and I would tiptoe, and the dog would be barking and growling, and I was grateful for that because I thought that would mask the sound of my footsteps coming up the stairs. Every time I would get to the top of the stairs, the noise would stop. The shutter clattering would stop. The footsteps were gone and you couldn't hear them anymore. I would go back downstairs, and sometimes it would start up again, and every time I would go up those stairs the noises would stop.

Eventually, I reconfigured the house, as you can see from the photos I have shown you. I tore out the old horsehair plaster, and tore out the ceilings, and I insulated it. I found some very interesting things in the walls—an old shoe and a lot of newspaper that was glued to the walls. I guess that was someone's attempt to insulate the house. I tore the house down to the frame, and I left the wide boards on the outside of the house, and ripped out the old windows that were 1940s vintage. I replaced all those house parts with new ones that were consistent with the vintage of this house. I took off the old asbestos siding and put on clapboards. I put in wooden windows and wooden storm windows. We had to rebuild part of the center chimney, which came from the old railroad round house in Augusta, so we had vintage bricks that we could put in the house. Also, they were put in with very narrow mortar joints, which was typical of houses from this period, not that wide mortar; a special combination that you have to make for the bricks to adhere to one another. I found a mason who knew how to do that, and so he built the center chimney. We eventually rebuilt the ell of the house as well. After everything was torn apart and everything was put back together with new products, those noises disappeared. I never heard from that spirit again.

The strange part of it all was that when I felt or heard the presence of the spirit, I never felt any fear. I never felt, whatever the presence was in that old house, that it intended any harm toward me. I just felt that whatever it was, it wasn't able to move on.

*Chapter 32*

# The Oellers House in Winthrop

*I first became acquainted with ghosts at the home of my best childhood friend, Elizabeth, nicknamed "Boo." Overlooking beautiful Maranacook Lake in Winthrop, the Oellers family lived in the 1818 Federal-style house at the top of Main Street. Boo and I have lost touch over the years, as she moved out of the state long ago. I recently reminisced with Rick Oellers, Boo's older brother, when he was on his annual summer vacation in Wayne. We referred to the ghost as "Mr. Sager," a name we heard from somewhere as being the former owner.*

Rick shared many stories about the old house:

There are lots of people who grew up with us, who witnessed many things there. My father, and my mother, who has passed away, would never admit to anything going on there with ghosts, though. However, I can think of many scary things that happened there. I don't even know where to start! Some things are really funky.

When we first moved in, I had the scariest room in the house,

165

because I had the attic door going from my bedroom. I remember that the door would come swinging open on its own, all the time. I would hear clunks and clatters, and maybe it was just settling some of the time... but, boy, I was terrified of that attic door! I would just stare at that door, and say, "Oh, don't you open again tonight!"

That attic door was the bane of my existence! Of course, there were many times I would see the dog sitting on the floor and appearing to watch someone walk across the room. That kind of stuff was just a normal happening.

I think one of the best stories was when my friends Doug, Jim, Chuck, and I were doing an overnight in the living room, and my parents were gone for the night. I was probably fourteen or fifteen years old, and we had a fresh blanket of snow outside. We were sitting around telling ghost stories and stuff, and the usual creaks and groans of the old house were getting us pretty scared. Then Doug went into the kitchen to get something to eat, and shortly thereafter, there was a knocking at the window, and we could see a hand waving in front of the window! We said, "Oh, knock it off, Doug, we know it's you!"

Doug came walking out from the kitchen with a sandwich in his hand, saying, "What are you guys talking about?" So, of course, we all were just flipping out! We all ran to the window and looked out, and of course, there were no footprints in the snow below the window. We were sure we saw, very clearly, a hand waving in the window. There was no doubt about it, as we all saw it.

That same night, Jim heard a sound in the closet. He opened the door, and he was so terrified he ran out of the house and he never came back. Sadly, he passed away about ten years after that, and had never told anyone what he saw. It was the den closet door, right outside the kitchen. He had run all the way home in the snow that night. We tried to ask him about it later, but he never wanted to talk about it. He would never tell us what he saw. He passed away young, tragically, at about age twenty-seven, and Doug, sadly, passed away very young, too. So, it's Chuck and I who are left for witnesses, unfortunately, on that one.

Another spooky thing happened in the barn. Now, the house is about two hundred years old. The barn is about one hundred feet away from the house. There is a carriage house connecting the house and the barn, which had been made into apartments. So, to get from the house to the barn, there is a long walkway. Just walking down the walkway was terrifying. In the attic space above the walkway, there was an old chopping block with an ax in it. The ax was really wedged deeply in the chopping block, which by the way, came with the house. Now, I could never get the ax out. The horse stable was close to this chopping block.

Sometimes my sister Beth, a.k.a. Boo, was too scared to go out to the barn by herself. Well, every morning when we would go out to feed the horse, the ax would be lying beside the chopping block on the floor. Every time. My sister Boo would testify to this. So one day, I had had enough, and I took the ax and I wedged it deeply into the chopping block with a sledgehammer. When we went out the next day, the chopping block was upside down! Really weird!

Well, these kinds of things went on for years. Just minor stuff. And there were other things. One time I remember watching a lightning storm, and there was this huge bolt of lightning. I remember seeing this image of an old man's face left on the window. I realized later on, when I was grown up and looking back on it, that it was probably a reflection of my own face in the window. Some stuff could be explained, I'm sure. There had to be a certain element of our imaginations going wild sometimes.

When I was about sixteen years old, I decided to move out into the passageway rooms in the carriage house. Around May first of that year, I moved out there, and had the whole place to myself. At that time I was in a rock 'n' roll band. The first few nights were just miserable; it was scary out there near the barn. There were so many bumps and creaks and noises. Even though I knew there was a horse out there in the barn that could be making some of the noises, it could be pretty creepy.

Well, about the third night I had come home, and I was getting pretty tired of this, and I admit I had been partying a little bit. I sat on the edge of my bed, and I said out loud, "Okay, we're going to have a little chat!" and I proceeded to go on for about a half an hour, basically having a conversation with the ghost. Basically saying how it's going to be, who I am, the law, you know, Kumbaya! From that night on, as far as the nasty stuff, it all ended.

There still was some stuff going on—for example, I had a stereo system that kept turning itself down. It was weird, because I would have the stereo cranked, and I'd leave the room and come back, and it would be turned down. It wasn't my dad, because he wasn't around at the time. So, I concluded that the ghost did not like loud music.

In fact, we all began to talk about the ghost like he was a family member. We called him Mr. Sager, because we had heard that the man who lived here before us had that name, and that he had died in this house. That's how legend had it.

I had a friend named Peter who came up from Massachusetts and stayed with us for almost a month. He slept in one of the other rooms in the passageway, and he started noticing the stereo turning down by itself. I explained that it was just Mr. Sager, the family ghost, and not to worry about it. He thought this was hilarious.

Peter began to bad-mouth Mr. Sager, and he even began to dare him to do things. Now, my bedroom used to have black light posters all over the walls. From the moment that Peter came to stay, every morning when he got up, he would step on a thumbtack. It got to the point when he woke up in the morning, and he would look around before getting out of bed! He would go to the bathroom, and when he came back to bed, he would step on one! It was just so bizarre, and I would say to him, "I told you not to mess with the ghost!"

During my senior year in high school, there were some bullies who lived up near Metcalf Road. Well, I was a smart mouth then, and I got myself in trouble once in a while. The bullies—Steve, Randy, and a couple others from up the road—were waiting to catch the bus home. I took the bus home once in a while when I was too lazy to walk up the hill. The bus driver, Mr. Morgan, didn't mind. So, these bullies were running to catch the bus, and I guess the bus driver didn't see them, and as we went by, I sort of gave them the bird out the window. I laughed because the bus took off without them. I guess they managed to steal some bikes or something, because they were there waiting for me at my house when the bus stopped!

When I got off the bus, Steve wanted to duke it out with me. I said, "Hey man, I don't want to fight with you." My sister's boyfriend, Brian, was there, and he witnessed this as well. I am not a fighter, I never was a fighter, and besides, I can't see that well. He came up behind me, and sucker-punched me in the head. I swung around and made a large swing, but I didn't touch a thing. I missed by a mile! Well, Steve flew back and landed on his butt hard, like someone had knocked the wind out of him! He got up, claiming somebody punched him where it counts, and he just cried, and ran away. I never laid a hand on the guy!

Well, to this day I wish I could ask him what really happened, because he never messed with me again. And every time he rode by on the bus, he would look over at me, and it was like we both knew that something happened that day. No one wants to admit it, but I am convinced in my mind that something hit him hard enough to knock him on his butt, and it was not me. I never hit him that day.

I went inside, and Brian said, "What did you do to him? He flew up in the air and fell back down on the ground!" I told him I didn't do anything.

After that, I got in the habit of talking to Mr. Sager, saying, "Hey, man, what's happening, Mr. Sager?" I really treated him, and thought of him, like a family member, you know? I wasn't really scared of him anymore. If I heard noises in the night, I'd say, "Hey Mr. Sager, how's it going?"

Ricky and I reminisced about our experiences at the house. We both remembered that the dogs were often staring at the ghost. I told Ricky that I too remembered the spooky passageway to the barn, and that Boo and I used to spend the night out there a lot. We were like amateur Ghostbusters, or so we thought, back then. We believed in ghosts, and it was fun, I admit, being scared and getting our adrenaline going.

I told Ricky about one experience that stood out in my mind as one of the creepiest, that I didn't think anyone was capable of causing. Boo and I were sleeping out in one of the rooms in the passageway. We were staying up late and giggling and talking. As soon as we turned the ceiling light out with the long string, so we could go to sleep, we would suddenly hear banging on the walls, then on the floor, then from above the ceiling; one right after the other! There was even banging from under the floor! We were terrified! Every time that we would hear the banging, we would pull the light switch string to "on," and the noise would stop. We'd pull ourselves together, and when we turned the light off, it would begin again. The light was off and on practically all night. To make matters worse, there were objects flying across the room and hitting us on the bed! We were just screaming!

I always remembered, after every night we spent either in the barn or in the passageway, that we would run back into the house in the morning, and we'd burst into the kitchen, anxious to tell Boo's parents everything that had happened to us during the night.. Ricky told me that the first few nights he ever spent out in the passageway, when it first became his bedroom, the exact same experiences happened to him. He had heard the same tapping and knocking sounds on the floors, ceiling, and walls and so on, and it terrified him as well. Weird.

We talked about the attic and the large door to the attic in Ricky's bedroom, with a steep stairway up, and a poorly lit and large attic space. I remember it as having many racks of hanging clothes, which obstructed one's view of things. On the rare occasion we went up there, it was only to find things like baby doll clothes or something. I definitely remember still the creepy, scary feeling, just being in that attic.

Ricky and I discussed the little things that went on there on a daily basis. I don't think there was ever a day I spent there with Boo that we didn't experience something spooky. Now, I realize there is an element of children having vivid imaginations, and we were caught up in the whole ghost experience, of course. I remember the large formal hall and stairway that led to the second floor, and Boo and I would just sit on the stairs sometimes and watch gray shadows move on the wallpapered walls. Now, maybe they were natural shadows from the tree branches swaying in the wind outside the windows. I don't know, but that stairway always had an eerie feeling for me.

I shared with Ricky another memory I have of playing up in the barn one day. Boo and I were setting up a puppet show or some kind of event that we were putting on for the neighborhood. We used to put on plays, and even magician shows, using the trap doors in the barn for making things disappear, and so on. I just remember that it was during the day, and as we were playing, we were suddenly frightened because we could hear what sounded like banging on the roof of the passageway. The unexplained banging was moving, like someone was pounding a hammer from the barn roof the whole distance of the entire passageway to the house. Of course, we were very frightened!

And, as often happened, we went running and screaming, all the way down the driveway to the house.

The Oellers' house made a definite impression on me as a child, to say the least! Really, I did love that old house. All of the hauntings that we experienced were, I think, the ghost being playful with us. It was like the ghost, Mr. Sager, was always teasing us. Yes, growing up and playing in that house with my best friend Boo made my childhood very rich indeed. Ricky and I remembered that there were many kids and neighborhood friends who became believers in ghosts, from spending time at that house back in the 1960s and 70s.

*Chapter 33*

# The Kosma's Ghost Experiences

*After I gathered the Oellers story, I stopped by the house to speak with the present owners, Dick and Pat Kosma, and I was excited to hear that they felt the house was haunted, too. Annette and Paula, my psychic friends, and I had a great evening meeting and talking with Dick and Pat. For me it was a trip back in time, to be in the presence of this awesome old house again.*

We walked into the kitchen first, and Annette said she immediately sensed that a doctor had lived there. As we walked into the large and formal living room, Annette also sensed a female presence. Dick told us that he often sees a female ghost passing by him in the house, out of the corner of his eye.

Annette told us that when there is a ghost in the house, it is often a woman, because women are usually the ones who become attached to their homes. "The woman usually does the decorating, and she is the one with the nesting instinct, because she is the heart of the home."

To get to the living room we passed through the formal dining

173

room, and Annette wanted to return to that room because she said she felt something very emotional there. The dining room, which has a tall ceiling and beautifully wallpapered walls, has two large built-in cabinets and a large dining room table in the middle of the room.

"I got very emotional when I came through here, and I wanted to cry. They (my spirit guides), make me feel things that sometimes convey what is going on or what happened at that time. I don't know if you know the history or not, but I am getting that someone passed away at this table at some point in time. I definitely feel that there was a man sitting right over there, and I believe he passed away at dinnertime, believe it or not."

Pat said that, oddly, her daughter never wants to eat in this dining room when she comes to visit.

Annette continued, "I am definitely getting that there was a very tall, thin man, who was frail, and he passed away at the table during dinnertime. I don't know if he had a heart attack, or what it was. Sometimes a house can have an echo or an imprint from something far back in the past, and maybe your daughter was picking up on that, as well as picking up on other people who once lived here."

In the living room, Dick told us more about the female ghost that he had seen passing by him all the time. "I feel a very strong presence all the time. I don't actually see her, but I know it is always a woman."

Paula said she could see a female ghost or spirit. "She's dressed like she is from the 1940s, the way her hair is pulled back. When you mentioned the man passing away at the table, I could hear her saying, 'That's because he never listens to me!'"

Annette said that she couldn't really tell what period the tall, thin man was from, but she noticed that he was dressed formally, wearing a suit made from a very thin material.

Paula said that the female she could see was also very dressed up.

We found the history of the house to be very interesting, which Pat read to us from the following article whose author is unknown:

The house reflects the elegance of the early 1800s. The early settlers of this community chose the sites to build their homes first, and then built the roads to reach them. The commanding view of the two lakes apparently influenced the builder of this fine residence on Hinds Hill, now known as "The Homestead," a tourist home. The house is located at the intersection of Augusta Road and Old Country Road, which once was known as the Meeting House Road. This section was the first to be settled in the town.

Built in 1817, the Homestead had been fortunate in its owners, and has come through the years well. The buildings are as sound and sturdy as when they went up, over a century and a half ago, and include a ten-room house, a barn, and a sixty-foot connecting runway. They rest on a foundation of solid granite blocks, all carried by an ox team from the Hallowell Quarry.

The history of Winthrop says this house was among the most prestigious and expensive in the town. Renovations have been made over the years; a porch has been added, and the white fence which once surrounded the property has been removed. Care has been exercised, however, and most of the original features have been preserved. The front entrance still holds its original etched-pane glass doors. Fireplaces in the den and living room have black marble faces outlined in white painted wood, and resemble those in the well-known Wiscasset Inn. A mahogany stairwell leads to the second floor, where all the floors have the original boards.

Dr. Snell, the first owner, was a direct descendent of Anna Alden, the granddaughter of John Alden of the Plymouth Colony. Dr. Snell settled here in 1806, and practiced medicine. Subsequent owners included James Wood, a retired sea captain, Francis Webb, a lawyer, and more recently the family of George Pike. Mrs. Elliott Sager, the present owner, and her late husband, came here to Winthrop from Portland in 1951. They purchased the property for a home, and soon after, opened it to tourists. Mrs. Sager subsequently added a gift and apparel shop, which soon outgrew the house and moved to the barn, which was remodeled to make it suitable. Mrs. Sager supervised the renovations in the barn, where only necessary changes were made. Sliding doors in the horse stalls, the hay chute from an overhead loft, and wide floorboards still are intact, and all the timbers, which were hand-hewn.

During my childhood years playing here, we always called the ghost "Mr. Sager," and I was a little surprised to hear that there actually was a Mr. Sager, who probably did pass away in the house, as the article implies that Mrs. Sager was widowed while living here.

Pat showed us a picture of her mother when she was young, and Paula said that the hairstyle of Pat's mother was exactly the hairstyle of the ghost or spirit lady that she was seeing. Paula told us that the woman she was seeing wanted her to ask Pat who Martha was. Pat was astounded, and explained that Martha was a neighbor of theirs who was an alcoholic, and who did crazy things. For example, she had locked herself in their car once. Pat said that she and her mother used to love to laugh over stories about this woman, Martha. Paula repeated that the woman who was standing in the corner kept saying, "Ask her about Martha, asked her about Martha!" Pat clearly felt that Paula was communicating with her mother's spirit.

We went into the old den which is now used as a bedroom, near the marble fireplace, and Annette said, "The Doctor says the andirons are missing." Dick was now the one astounded!

"I just took them out last week!" Dick said, "Wow, they're out in the barn! How did you know that? That's weird. I can't believe that!"

Annette said, "He wants you to put them back. Were they original to the home?"

Dick said he thought they were. Very strange.

Upstairs in a front bedroom, Annette was picking up some sadness. "I'm getting that there was a woman whose husband died before her, and though she was a strong woman, she was very lonely without him. I think she is the same woman that Dick sees who is wearing a flowing dress."

As we walked down the beautiful staircase, we stopped at the large landing, and Annette told us that her spirit guides were telling her that there was a mural painted on this wall. We wondered if there was really a mural underneath the wallpaper from years ago. As we were talking there, Annette could see the tall, thin man coming down the stairs behind me. She described him as being very frail and carrying a cane in one hand.

"I have to ask my spirit guides if I am looking at the past; a person who once existed, or am I seeing a ghost that is here now? They are telling me that I am seeing him from the past, and that he is a spirit and his grieving wife is a ghost, the woman with the flowing dress. I'm seeing him coming down the stairs and he's not aware of us, and he doesn't see us. I am seeing him in another time. Cathy was in his way, but I didn't see Cathy; I just saw him coming down the stairs. "

As we walked up the driveway toward the barn, Annette said that the woman was putting her hands around her neck. Laughing, Annette said, "I asked her, 'Why are you doing this?'"

"She said, 'My husband...'"

"Oh, your husband! He choked to death?"

"'Yes!'"

Annette explained to us that the woman ghost was trying all along to say that her husband choked to death at the dining room table!

It has been rumored for many years that this house, and the old Dooling place across the street, both had an Underground Railroad tunnel system, but Mr. Oellers had told me he could never find evidence of one anywhere. Dick had previously told me he thought there appeared to be a tunnel that went from the barn and down the driveway, and appeared to go up to the road in the direction of the site of the old Dooling house, which had long ago been torn down. The tunnel area is evidenced by a mounded and cracked appearance of the tar along the driveway. We asked Annette when we were in the house earlier if she sensed anything about an Underground Railroad. She said she was getting that the barn was involved, not the house, and that the barn in fact, was the entranceway.

Pat told us that she has had a strange experience when walking out behind the barn past her property near her neighbor's field. "I just feel this scary feeling, like the fight-or-flight response you get, you know? I feel like I would if there's a fox or something around, when I have the dogs with me. I feel really threatened for no reason at all, out there."

Annette said, "I wonder if it's related to the Underground Railroad, because of course they would have had that fight-or-flight feeling if they were approaching or exiting this house from the woods. The exit point may have been in the woods, as they never would have dared run across an open field. It makes sense to me that Pat is picking up the energies from that time."

Dick told us, "The other night I was watching television in the living room, and Pat had gone to bed, but I couldn't sleep. I smelled perfume. It wasn't what Pat wears and it wasn't anything that smells new, like "Jessica Savage" or something like that. It was like more of an older woman's perfume. A little while later it came back again. I started laughing, and thought, 'Where is this all coming from?'"

It was wonderful to meet the Kosmas and to see the house again. It was great to finally learn some of the history of this house, and to hear the impressions about the hauntings from Annette and Paula.

*Chapter 34*

# Monmouth Hauntings

*The following story is a reprint of a paper written by Bobbi Bowler for the Monmouth Museum, Inc., October 1989:*

## Ghost Legends of Monmouth

Fall is in the air, the winds carry the whispers and moans of lost souls, and soon Halloween will be upon us. It is at this time of year one recalls the ghost stories of one's childhood. In *Cochrane's History of Monmouth and Wales* I have often read the ghastly tale of Asenath White's ghost, and wondered what other eerie stories lurk about untold.

The first tale of uncanny nature concerns the Joseph R. King house in North Monmouth. Joseph R. King was a prominent manufacturer in North Monmouth. He was commemorated by the watering trough, which was erected in 1916. His son, Albertus R. King, married Ella Ramsdell on February 27, 1876. It is the ghost of Ella Ramsdell that is said to haunt the old King house.

Ella is said to have been a very beautiful woman, but as she became older she never let anyone see her face. When she went out, she wore a broad-brimmed hat and a heavy veil. Some people would say she was afraid the sunlight would mar her beauty, and others say she had been disfigured. It has been said that, while the house was occupied by Gordon Lindsey, Ella would take Mr. Lindsey's hat and place it on his bedpost upstairs. It has also been said that, when the house was empty, several people saw a figure at the windows.

Another tale concerns the old Jeffrey house in North Monmouth. Jesse Jeffrey served in Company B of the 5th Maine Regiment during the Civil War. He lost his right arm at the Battle of Spotsylvania Court House in May of 1864. After the Civil War he became a lawyer and moved to North Monmouth in 1878, where he held his practice. His legal file cabinet can be seen in the Monmouth Museum's Stencil Shop. Jesse Jeffrey died September 4, 1901, and his son W. Percy Jeffrey remained on at the old homestead. Percy Jeffrey is said to have been quite the character. People used to joke about the fact that Percy used to milk his cows at midnight and noon. Percy Jeffrey died January 12, 1970. It has been said that his ghost has been the reason behind the number of occupants to own the house since his passing. People residing in the house in the years since Percy's death have reported seeing the figure of an old man in a shawl, rocking in the kitchen in the late afternoon.

One of the Fairbanks' old houses in North Monmouth has been the reported home of several ghosts. The ghosts which have been reported as having made an appearance over a period of several years were that of a cat, a man dressed in 1800s attire, and a woman with her hair pinned up, wearing a long dress with a ruffle around the top. In 1868, just before Christmas, the figure of a woman was reported to be seen walking through the living room to the stairway door. The woman then opened the door, entered the hallway to the stairs, and closed the door behind her.

Around this same time, it was reported that one night the sound of high heels was heard going down into the cellar. The ghost of a man (reported seen during the winter) was seen in the kitchen. He had big sideburns and a sparse beard. He wore a dark blue Scotch Cap with ear flaps, a bill, and a pompom on top. He wore small steel-rimmed spectacles and a long coat with a double row of large dark buttons. He also wore a pair of long driving mittens. He was reported seen by a woman, who, when she turned around and then turned back, found him vanished. The woman noted that it had been snowing outside

and that there was no puddle on the floor where the man had stood.

During warmer weather, a woman in a black dress was reportedly seen at the top of the stairs, where she would walk towards the door. The cat was reportedly seen in the hallway, along the side of the stairs, where it would walk towards the door. The cat was large, short-haired, black, and lean. It would be there one minute and gone the next. The ghosts of the Fairbanks house have not been seen for several years, and it is supposed that they found the occupants of the household a little tedious and moved on to a more challenging environment.

I am sure there are countless ghost stories and other uncanny tales that lie buried in the memories of the residents of Monmouth and Wales. The stories of Harry Cochrane's ghost occupying the auditorium of Cumston Hall have been passed on from days when the Monmouth Repertoire Company played upon the stage there. It is always fun to jog one's imagination with a little unnatural history. So beware, on Halloween Night, if you are driving on Blue Ridge Road heading towards town, you may see history repeat itself with the return of Asenath White's ghost.

Note: The original story of Asenath White's ghost can be found in *Cochrane's History of Monmouth and Wales.*

photograph courtesy of The Kosma Family

Chapter 35

# The King House in Monmouth

*Pat Kosma of Winthrop told me that her late parents, Lorene and Gordon Lindsay, owned the old King House in Monmouth from about 1969 to about 1982. Pat said, "My father and some people he grew up with had all come back to the area, and they had told my parents a lot of the stories about the house being haunted." Pat and her husband Dick remember well the very spooky home.*

Dick said, "The house was really neat. The summer kitchen had a honeycomb fireplace in it that they baked in. There was a bathtub out there, and if you lifted the cover on it, it was all copper inside. There were fourteen rooms in that house, and Lorene and Gordon did a great job restoring it."

There are a couple of different versions of the story about the famed ghost, known to many townsfolk as Ella. (See previous Monmouth Hauntings story.) Dick and Pat's niece, Lisa, had lived there for a couple of years with her grandparents when she was young. Lisa remembered well the strong feeling of Ella's presence in the home.

She had always heard that Ella, who was the daughter of Joseph King, had hanged herself.

Pat told us she had also heard this story. "Ella was Joseph King's daughter, and she had a miscarriage, and she grieved so much that she just lost her mind. Her parents were embarrassed about it, so they kept her upstairs in the house all the time."

Dick added, "Remember that rope that was hanging from the beam, which looked like it was cut? It was weird, so nobody would touch it. Even my father-in-law said, 'Leave it alone, it's not bothering anybody.'" We all agreed that there was probably some truth somewhere in the stories.

Dick began the story about the first time he and Pat went there to stay, in the winter, many years ago: We drove up from Connecticut, and on the night we arrived there, just Pat and I, we put some mattresses down and lit the fire. That night was the strongest we ever felt of Ella's presence there. Somebody definitely was walking down those stairs; both of us heard it. Then a door slammed shut upstairs, and that would lift you right off from your bed! We knew we were the only ones there, and we knew that door didn't just slowly shut with the wind. It slammed shut! We certainly felt like she just wanted us to leave. One time I had had a little wine and was feeling brave, and walked over to the door and opened it quickly. There was no one in there, of course.

Pat continued: We were just scared to death! I kept saying, "Why are we here!?" It was a get-away weekend for us. My mother had the kids. But it was so scary. It was like watching one of those horror movies where you wonder, "Why don't they get out of there?" We were laughing, but it was as scary as could be. There were really loud knocking sounds, and we felt she (Ella) didn't want us there. As the years went on, the house stopped feeling so malevolent. It felt less angry. I don't know if it was us, or if we learned to live with it and just say, "Oh, that's just Ella," and accept her and not be so frightened.

Dick added: Your mother had such a great sense of humor—she would call Ella, and clap her hands, and so on! She was just wonderful!

We had a friend in Connecticut named Fred, who was a big burly red-headed Irish kid, with freckles all over him. He was a pretty smart kid. We all loved him and he was a good friend. We invited him to go up to Maine with us, to stay at the house. Fred would walk around the whole house, just kind of wobble and stuff. He was just a great guy, and after a while we all went to bed. Fred slept in a back bedroom upstairs. There were four bedrooms upstairs, and Pat's parents slept in a bedroom downstairs. Well, he got up in the morning, and he was just white!

Pat continued the story: Now, first of all, he was a good Catholic kid, so he didn't really buy into the ghost stuff. Yet he told us that a couple of times in the night, he felt this pressure on his chest, like someone was sitting on him. The first time he said it was almost like he would feel this pressure and he couldn't even get up. Then it lifted, and he said he got up and went in the bathroom and washed his face, and walked around for a minute. He went back to bed, and after about a half hour, it happened again. He was just in shock. He just left that morning and went back to Connecticut!

Dick: There was a front stairway, and in the back there were maid's quarters, which had a stairway that went first into a hallway, then a summer kitchen. It was there you could feel a presence that was very strong. That stairway also led in to the top of the (attached) barn. That place would just make the hair on the back of your neck stand up!

Our son, even when he was very young, would never sleep upstairs in that house. We called him "Radar" because he would say something, and soon after, somebody would show up, or something would happen. For example, we would be talking about him, and then soon after the phone would ring and it would be him. It just happened way too much. His friends call him "Radar," too. So in that house we all felt something; but he was really aware of it.

Oh, things happened all the time. Things were moved around a lot. For example, something that you have would go missing. You knew you left it there. Later, after looking for it everywhere, it would be right there in plain sight where you left it in the first place. She (Ella) really drove Pat's mother crazy sometimes. One time on New Year's Eve, she (Ella) even popped the champagne cork. It was just sitting there, and all by itself the cork popped!

Pat: My father died in 1979, and my mother stayed here for about three years after that. We had moved to Maine in 1978, and lived in Windsor for a couple of years, and then we moved to Readfield. In

1982 my mother moved to Readfield to be closer to us. My mother had a photograph that she took while standing in the driveway looking up at one of the upstairs windows. There is an image in the window of a woman's face. It was winter, and there was frost on the window, and in the frost is an image of a face looking out the window. My mother loved that picture, she was so proud of it! Unfortunately, the picture has been missing for years.

Though it was very scary, the Kosmas certainly have very fond memories of that very special house.

*photograph courtesy of Mary Jane Dillingham*

*Chapter 36*

# The Dragonfly Shop in Litchfield

*Annette and I visited the Dragonfly Shop in Litchfield to meet Mary Jane Dillingham, whose shop reportedly had ghosts. This large antique barn has been beautifully restored and kept as a gift and antiques shop. The barn originally was located across the street, and Mary Jane said the barn has actually been moved three times. The old farmhouse was built in 1860. The following is an account of our visit with Mary Jane, an artist and a most interesting woman.*

Mary Jane told us she has noticed many objects in her shop being moved around, and there have been ghost sightings in the shop, too. Annette was able to give details and explanations which were right on the mark, according to Mary Jane.

When we first arrived, Mary Jane gave Annette a large spike to hold, which she explained had just appeared one day in her shop lying on a table. Annette immediately got the impression of a man associated with this spike. Annette said the man knew she was coming, and he was waiting to tell her his story.

"Sometimes a ghost will move things to get your attention," Annette told Mary Jane. "They have their stories to tell, and this man is somehow connected to the railroad. He is very sad, and he is saying that he was in an accident. This place is filled with so many antiques, and you have many ghosts and spirits attached to them. These ghosts are attached to their belongings, so even though you are selling these antiques, they (the ghosts) are staying with them. It is definitely very active here; very active. But they come and go, they are telling me."

"Do you sense any presence here now?" Mary Jane wanted to know.

Annette laughed and said, "I think you have a whole crowd here! Because of your antiques in the shop, there are many ghosts, and I can see them, and they are all standing here watching us, and waiting to talk to me. I can see one or two over there; I can't see some of their faces, but they are there. I see a man over there, and a woman standing right here in the forefront."

"Does she have a pink bonnet on?"

"Yes, she is coming through," said Annette, "and her bonnet is pink. She is saying that her bonnet is like sunscreen to you and me."

"One of the ladies who worked for me in the shop had seen the ghost of a woman who was very thin and frail looking, and was wearing a pink bonnet. She likes what I'm doing with the shop."

Mary Jane told us that her daughter-in-law had been standing in this spot recently, and looked up at a mannequin on an open level of the barn, and she saw a man standing there. Mary Jane initially asked her what she had been drinking!

"She said she saw a gentleman in overalls, standing up there."

Annette said she could see him and described the ghost as very thin, and she said this ghost was connected to the original farmhouse. Mary Jane said that the ghost could be a member of the True family. Annette asked Mary Jane to look into this man, and see if he was connected to the railroad.

We went upstairs among the antiques, and Annette was attracted to an old chair, and she said she sensed that there had been a murder. "It actually was an accident, and a man was shot through the heart."

Mary Jane said she knew something about this, because the consignor had told her a man had been shot while sitting in that chair.

She was not sure if the man had actually died or not. Annette thought that the man was standing up when he was shot, and then he fell back into the chair, and that he died a couple of hours later. Mary Jane said she was concerned when she heard the story, and she almost didn't put the chair in her shop. She had heard that the murder victim was a teenager, and that he had been shot in the back, but she wasn't sure if it was true or not.

Annette was getting the words, "Didn't mean to shoot him, only meant to scare him." Annette insisted that she thought it was an accident, and that there was no negative energy around the chair like there would have been if it had been a murder situation. The ghost came through, and told Annette that he was not a victim, and he also stressed that it was an accident.

"Do you pick up anything else?" Mary Jane asked.

Annette laughed and said, "Yeah, there's quite a few here waiting to tell me their stories."

Annette said there was another murder connected to something among the antiques, and she walked over toward an old felt hat, which looked like the hat a Boy Scout would wear, from years ago. "I'm getting heavy and sad," Annette said. She told us the hat was also involved in a murder, though she wasn't sure if someone had been wearing it during a murder, but that it was somehow involved. "I'd burn that hat," she told Mary Jane. Mary Jane did just that.

Annette said that she thought she would like to come back in the spring, when it's warmer in the barn, and bring a pencil and pad of paper. She said there were so many ghosts and spirits with so many stories to tell, but that it was too cold for her to stay in the barn for long on that day.

Annette said that she was getting that a lot of farmers were connected to a lot of the stuff in the barn. Mary Jane told us that a lot of her antiques had come from her grandparents' estate, and that they were indeed farmers. Annette said she saw a ghost sitting in a chair in the shop, and that he was all dressed up, in church clothes. She asked Mary Jane if he sounded like her grandfather. Mary Jane said it could be her other grandfather, who wasn't a farmer. Annette said that this man was wearing a charcoal-colored suit coat, and that he could be from anywhere.

Before Annette left the barn, she kept insisting that she was feeling a sad feeling from some object here. As she walked around and tried to identify which object it was, she said that she really felt it was the woman in the pink bonnet that was giving her the feeling of sadness somehow. "I think her story is tragic," Annette said.

Mary Jane invited us into her beautifully restored old farmhouse, which she said was also built around 1860. Annette immediately got the word "suede," and asked Mary Jane what that could mean. Mary Jane answered that she had just bought some suede textured paint that she was intending to put on the walls. Mary Jane said it was a colonial red color.

Annette said there was a ghost lady standing in the corner saying that she liked it. Annette remarked that she felt like she had to ask permission before she walked into the rooms, and she explained that the ghost lady was a former owner of the home. "The woman just exudes manners," Annette said.

Mary Jane told Annette that when her daughter-in-law had been staying with her recently, she had a cat, and that cat would not go up the stairs. She said her own cats go up the stairs, but that this cat appeared to be afraid to go up the stairs. Annette could see a ghost on the landing at the top of the stairs, who she described as gruff, and said that he did not like cats. The ghost told Annette that he had lived in this house at one time, but not for very long. Annette got the impression that he had been a boarder here, and he conveyed to her that he was just passing through. Mary Jane validated that information by saying she had heard that there were boarders who lived there long ago.

Annette told us she could still see the ghost lady, who told her that the particular room which we were in had been altered. Mary Jane validated that it was indeed altered, and that she herself did not like it, and planned to tear down the plastic molding and replace it. Annette said that the lady agreed with Mary Jane, and in fact she liked Mary Jane quite a bit. She liked what Mary Jane had done with the house, and was very pleased. Annette said that this lady said she was the first owner of the house.

Mary Jane replied, "That must be Mrs. True!"

Annette said that yes, the ghost lady said she was Mrs. True. "So let's call her Mrs. True, as she is very into etiquette!" Annette added that she really liked this lady, who had a very nice energy.

Mary Jane thought that the True family had lived here, then the Chesley family, and then there had been two ladies that lived here after that. Annette said that she was getting that one of them was a teacher. Mary Jane validated that she had heard that one of the sisters was a teacher. Mary Jane also said that this house at one time years ago had served as the Litchfield Post Office.

Annette described a teenager who was also coming through. She wasn't sure if he was from the 1800s or not. "I don't know if he came from the barn, with all the antiques, or if he is from this house," Annette said. "He came from this side of the house, from this direction. So, I guess he's trying to tell us he is not from the barn." He told Annette that he had drowned in the pond, which was somewhere out behind the house. Mary Jane explained that there was a pond out behind the house, near a place called Bachelder's Tavern.

Annette stressed that this was a very active house. "It is filled with ghosts and spirits, and it has a very good energy to it."

The ghost of Mrs. True repeated to Annette that she was very happy with how Mary Jane was taking care of the house. Annette said Mrs. True knew that she was a ghost, and that she needed to cross over, but that she wasn't ready to leave the house yet.

Mary Jane said that she has always been aware of things being moved to different places in the house. She asked if Mrs. True was doing this.

Annette said that sometimes it was Mary Jane's guardian spirits that were letting her know that they were around her. "They are just saying hello."

Mary Jane shared that there was a male presence that sometimes comes up to her bedroom at night, and wakes her. She said she wondered if she was just dreaming. She said that she can see his body but not his face. Annette got the word "actor" with him, and asked if that meant anything to Mary Jane.

Mary Jane told us that she was engaged to Marilyn Monroe's first husband, and that his name was Jim. She said that he had been a singer, and had once sung with the Jane Russell. Mary Jane said that he had died of leukemia just a few years ago, and that she had loved him very much. She also shared with us that when she was young she herself was a dead ringer for Marilyn Monroe. She had pictures which she showed us, and we certainly agreed.

Mary Jane showed us her weaving room upstairs, and Annette said that Mrs. True loved watching her weave in this room. Annette said the ghost lady was truly fascinated with Mary Jane. Her art studio was also fabulous.

When we went upstairs to Mary Jane's bedroom, Annette could see the spirit of a man sitting in a chair. The man kept his gaze on Mary Jane, Annette said. From Annette's description, Mary Jane confirmed that the man was her former husband, who had passed away a few years before. Annette said he loved Mary Jane very much, and that he had crossed over and was very happy that he was a spirit and just visiting.

Mary Jane also shared with us that she and her deceased former husband had owned a funeral home in Auburn, which was very haunted as well. They once had a visit, she said, from a paranormal group who also confirmed the activity there.

We found Mary Jane to be a very gifted and fascinating woman, and with quite a life story. We promised to return to the Dragonfly Shop barn in the spring, to explore more ghosts.

*Chapter 37*

## Annette's House in Temple

*Annette Parlin, our medium clairvoyant, lives in an old farmhouse in Temple. Annette and her husband Ronal are both talented artists and they have three grown children.*

*Annette has many, many beautiful stories about encounters with ghosts and spirits. I met her when on a visit to the haunted house called Greentrees, in Mount Vernon, and she has visited many haunted houses with me since. She has taught me many things about the spirit world, and has been an influence on my growing spirituality, and she has also become a good friend. I am amazed by her psychic gifts, and her ability to comfort those whom we visit. She is a very articulate speaker, and the following are some personal stories about her own haunted house:*

My husband and I put a tape recorder in our house, and left it going overnight to see if it would pick up any activity in the house. We put it in the barn studio where my husband does his work. I had not yet listened to it but my sister did, and then it got accidentally erased.

First, let me tell you that there used to be a blacksmith shop on the farm, and there were many cattle here, too, back in the 1800s. It was first sold in 1855 by a widow. I had always been told by my spirit guides that the house was built in 1828. We know that it is at least 1855, because of the records. So I myself wanted to do some research to find out exactly when it was built. Now, on this farm there was a huge cattle barn. And right near the house there was a blacksmith shop.

When my sisters, who are also very psychic, listened to the recording, they could hear sounds in the background that sounded like what you would hear in a blacksmith shop, which has been gone for probably a hundred years. You could hear the blacksmith working, and you could hear chains in the bellows that he used on the fire. Then you could hear him tinkering, tinkering, to the point where they could even hear him say, "Ouch!" once in a while. They could even hear what sounded like another person coming into the shop, and the murmur of their voices as they talked. How cool is that!

Another time, we left the recorder on at night when we went to bed. We knew we had several hours on the machine which would take it through the whole night. But when we got up in the morning, it was off. We thought this was weird; it shouldn't be off. It should be still running. Anyway, you can hear some women talking and laughing. Then, you could hear a man go, "Shhh!" You can hear on the recording someone coming closer and closer to the recorder, and then you hear it being picked up, and click! It goes off. Someone actually picked it up and stopped it!

This house was very active, especially in the years that my kids were growing up. We would see and hear things, and the kid's friends would also experience things. Oh, boy, I wish my kids were here to tell you this one because they might have a better recollection of how it happened. I have three kids, two boys and a girl.

One time when one of my sons was a teenager, he was here with a girlfriend, and my middle son was also here with a friend. It was late in the evening, around eleven or twelve o' clock, and they had been up watching TV. My son decided to go to bed. His friend was still hanging around, and he decided he would go to bed, too. Well, he (the friend) came out of the TV room and looked over toward the kitchen, down the hall, and he could see a shadow of someone. When he looked up, he saw this young man and he thought it was my son. The young man peered around the woodstove, and looked right at him, and then disappeared. Well, he thought it was my son Chad. He went into the kitchen and around the woodstove, and he thought, "I must have missed him." So he walked back down toward the living room, and he started to go up the stairs. He looked back down, and there was that person again, looking right at him. At that point, he ran up the stairs, and was even more freaked out when he saw my son sitting up in bed! He said, "You're supposed to be downstairs!" and Chad stated that he had been in his bedroom that whole time.

We later found out that there was a young ghost. We did cross him over, and we called him Benny. He was usually upstairs in the attic. There are three bedrooms upstairs, and the smallest bedroom is closest to the attic. Nobody ever wanted to sleep in that bedroom. It always gave everybody a creepy feeling. Well, it would always be in that bedroom in the attic that we could sense this young man. He probably always stayed up there because he was being polite. What we got from him was that he died young, in his twenties, from a hunting accident. He loved my boys, probably because he related to their age, and would always try to get their attention.

One time my son Chad was doing his homework in that bedroom, and he could hear something sliding across his bureau. He looked over, and he could actually see an empty cup as it slid across the bureau and landed on his bed. He got up and screamed, and ran out! We got that it was Benny and that he was trying to get Chad's attention and wanted to play with him.

My daughter has seen what she calls the "yellow people" in her room upstairs. Her first sighting she called an angel. She described her as emitting a yellow light, like a light bulb would. She said this angel had wings and was looking right at her. Then she saw two more of these yellow people, who she described as looking like princesses, which was the best she said that she could describe them. One of them was looking at her and the other one was looking at her friend, who was sleeping over. The one that was looking at her, she said, was wearing a crown and was holding flowers. I believe that must've been one of her spirit guides or something.

One day we heard what sounded like a woman humming. It was

Easter Sunday, and my husband wasn't home, so my kids and I went to visit their grandparents. When we came back home, the kids went into the house immediately, while I went out to tend to the horses in the barn. When I came into the kitchen, my son freaked out, and he said, "What are you doing here, you're supposed to be in your bedroom!"

I said, "No, I just came in from the barn; I haven't been in the house since we came home."

"I just talked to you in your bedroom."

"You did," I said laughing, "What did I say?"

"Your door was closed, so I assumed you were changing, and I said, 'Mom, when are we going to have dinner?' You were sort of mumbling, and I didn't really hear what you said, but you answered."

He said, "I didn't hear what you said, so I repeated, 'Mom when are we going to have dinner?'" And again he heard mumble, mumble, mumble. He gave up, and that's when I walked in the door at the other end of the house.

So, he freaked out, though I laughed, and said, "Maybe that was your grandmother joking with you!"

We would all hear and see things; lights that go on and off, doors that open and close. One time we had gone for the weekend, and I had asked a neighbor to take care of the animals for me. I asked her to come into the house once in a while and check to make sure that everything was okay in the house. It was wintertime, and so I told her I was going to just close the upstairs bedroom off so it wouldn't have to be heated. So when the weekend was over and we came home, I asked my neighbor how everything was.

She said, "Do you have ghosts in your house?" She said that she had gone upstairs and the door was open, so she closed the door, and when she came back to check it again later, one of the doors was open again. It got to the point where she was so scared that she brought her husband with her when she came over to take care of the animals and check on the house. She said that every time she came over, the doors were taking their turns being open!

We have heard doors open and close, and we have heard people walking in our house. My husband and I both have big families, and we have guests all the time. One time we had a full house, and one of my sisters was sleeping on the floor here. I In the middle of the night something woke her, and she could hear someone walking around in the kitchen. So, it has been a very, very active house, especially when the kids were here.

I know that my grandmother has always been here, because she is one of my main spirit guides. She died when my mother was a child, so I have never met her, but she is around all the time, letting us know that she is here, and we often hear pots and pans rattling and things like that. Sometimes we hear a "hello" or singing.

One time, I remember my son and I were coming home from somewhere, and we had arrived in separate cars. When I came into the house I could hear music playing, and it was guitar music, so I thought, "Oh, Chad is already playing his guitar." But I knew that I had beaten him home, and so I knew that there was no one else in the house.

When Chad came in, I asked him if his guitar was upstairs, and he said yes. I told him I had just heard the most beautiful music playing on his guitar. I told him it was just a few notes; it was four chords to a melody. I made him go upstairs and play it while I stood in the kitchen to see if I could hear the guitar playing from the kitchen. He had to play pretty loud up there for me to even hear it down in the kitchen.

We also have a ghost here whose name is Mr. Smith. He used to be someone who lived here on the farm, and we believe he was a hired helper. I knew about him, but I never said hello. I would see him when I went out to the barn to do chores and stuff, and I guess one time he got mad at me. I had gone away again one weekend, and when I came back, one of the fence posts was pulled aside in a way that I was not able to explain. I looked for footprints, and there were none, though the ground was very spongy and wet. I could only conclude that it was a spirit, but I was mad because now I had more work to do to repair it. I said out loud, "Is that you Mr. Smith?"

And I got, "You never say hi to me!"

So, I fixed the fence, and now every morning when I head out to the barn, I say, "Hi, Mr. Smith!"

I have even heard horses, but not my horses, in the pasture. For example, one time I was working my own horse in the arena, and I heard this other horse nicker. I looked at my other horse, and he was grazing, and I thought… he couldn't have made that nicker. He was eating, and he had a mouthful. Then I thought, "How odd!" So we kept riding, and all of a sudden I heard it again, and this time my horse heard it, too. I looked at my other horse, and he was just kind of minding his own business, and it just kind of freaked me out. I heard it three times, so I just got off my horse, put her away and left. I didn't know what to think of it.

About a week went by, and I was talking to my horses as I was brushing them. I was in between two horses, and I heard a nicker again, and the horses heard it, too, because all three of us looked over at the same time to see what it was. Now, a nicker is pretty soft; you have to be pretty close to a horse to hear it nicker. It was eerie to me because I was hearing a horse, and there was nothing there. I guess now I also have a spirit horse on my property!

I am told that there was another woman who lived here back when the house was first built. We call her Mary, and she is a heavy-set woman with a printed dress, and she lived here when there were lots of daffodils planted on this farm. I found it odd when we moved here that there were no lilacs, no flowers, and no rhubarb, like you normally find on an old farm. It was clean as a whistle, so we planted lots of flowers ourselves when we first moved here. But she is here, and she is also another one who rattles my pots and pans in the kitchen. She likes to stay out in the kitchen; that is her place. It seems like they all like to have their favorite places.

One time, I was lying here napping on the couch in the evening, and I woke up and I saw this man standing in the doorway. Now, he looked like a dark shadow to me. I didn't see any details yet, but I knew that he was looking right at me. I looked at him and I thought, "I know that nothing is going to harm me, and I must know this person," and I lay down and closed my eyes again. I couldn't go back to sleep, so I opened my eyes, and again, he was still there! It definitely bothered me, because he wasn't saying anything, and I didn't know who he was.

So I got up and walked right by him to go up to bed. I thought, "Okay, that was really different!" That was maybe twenty years ago, and I have grown as a psychic since then. Now I can get a much stronger sense of ghosts and spirits and who they are, and I am not afraid of ghosts or spirits at all anymore.

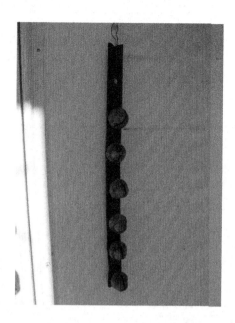

*Chapter 38*

# Sleigh Bells in Farmington

*My sister Nancy is definitely a skeptic when it comes to the idea of ghosts. However, she lived in an old farmhouse in Farmington several years ago, which was rumored to be haunted, and she found some things hard to explain or ignore. She and her former husband, Alan, did not want to solicit the ghost stories from the townspeople while they lived there. It was a very charming old farmhouse, and was reportedly built in 1874.*

I asked Nancy recently about the house because I vaguely remembered that she had mentioned some interesting stories years ago. She said that though they never actually saw anything, there were several occasions when they had heard weird noises in the house. It always sounded like someone was walking on the stairs, Nancy admitted.

Then there is the story about her son Jesse, who at the time was maybe four years old. She had sent him upstairs to his room for a timeout. He used to sit at the top of the steps when she sent him to his room, rather than go down the hall to his bedroom. This one time Nancy remembers that something really scared Jesse on the stairs, and he came running down visibly very frightened, with his eyes wide open, but too young to really explain what he had seen or heard. It had made an impression on Nancy, even though she didn't believe in ghosts at the time. Or she didn't want to believe.

She also recalls that she would frequently hear the sound of bells early in the morning while she lay in bed, and she would get up and go to the window, expecting to see a herd of goats in the yard with bells on, because that's just how it sounded, she said.

I called her former husband Alan, who at the time that they lived at the house worked as the Town Manager for Farmington. I asked him what he remembered about the old house. He confirmed Nancy's story that, "There was something about that house…" and the fact that they sometimes heard things they couldn't explain. He told me that he too remembered hearing bells in the night or early in the morning.

He said, "They sounded like those acorn-shaped bells that would be on a strap of leather."

I asked him if he had ever inquired about the house with anyone in town. Though it had been a while, he remembered that he had once talked to a man named Lewis Wright, who told him that he had been born in the house in the year 1900. He had told Alan that a family had lived there many years ago whose name he thought was Pinkham, and that they had come from North Chesterville, and that they had built sleighs for a living.

"I never really thought about this before!" he exclaimed, surprised that he had never before connected this information with the fact that he and Nancy had heard bells in the house. Now the thought of sleigh bells seemed to fit the mystery for him.

Alan also remembered hearing from people in town that the house was reportedly haunted by a young girl who had died there many, many years before. Oddly, Alan also remembered there was an old story that you could never put a bathtub in the house, and that the first man who tried it had had a heart attack. Then another owner had tried to put a bathtub in, and something else bad had happened to him. Funny how stories get started.

It seems some people are more open to ghostly experiences than others, but occasionally ghosts make themselves known anyway!

*Chapter 39*

# Ghosts in New Sharon

*It's amazing how many people have ghosts. More often than not, when I have mentioned to someone that I am collecting ghost stories, they know someone who has a ghost. Such was the case with my co-worker Vicki. She said her sister's home had ghosts. We arranged for a visit with Annette and Paula at the home of Vicki's sister Pam in New Sharon.*

Immediately, Annette felt a grandfather figure in the home. She said that he was wearing a hat and a suit coat, and that he was dressed sort of fancy. "Can you relate to that?" Annette asked Pam.

Pam nodded and emphatically said, "Yes."

Annette told us that when she was in the bathroom and she was looking at the pretty wallpaper, she felt the presence of a grandmother who told her that she loved the wallpaper! "She said she thinks it's very old-fashioned."

Pam replied that she was sure that Annette was talking about her son's grandfather on her ex- husband's side, and she explained that he had passed about a year before. Pam said that he was a wonderful man, and that she was very close to him. Pam also told us that he fit Annette's description very well. She said that he always wore hats and that he was a dentist and often wore a business suit. Pam, like many of the people we visited, preferred to see what Annette picked up before telling the details of her ghost stories.

"First of all," Pam began, "I was a non-believer, and I felt like there were common sense reasons for the things that happened. When I moved to this house, I was a single mom with three kids, and I did not need anything else going on! It all started the first night that we were here. My first night I was here alone, because my ex-husband had the children that night. I didn't feel scared, but I heard coughing. I thought, 'Oh, well, that must be a noise that the house makes.' I've heard it every now and again since; and that was about ten years ago. That was my first 'Geez, what was that?' moment. Then my basement door kept opening, and we fixed it. However, it just started happening again recently. I don't look for these things to happen, but it was like, 'Stop and think, did that really happen?'"

Paula spoke up and said, "I feel like it's a loved one from your side of the family."

Pam continued, "The basement door was open, and I said to my mother, 'Did you just open the basement door?' She answered, 'No, why would I open the basement door?' It has happened before, but this time it was completely wide open, and just prior to that, I had walked by and noticed it was closed. It was just my mother and me in my house."

Annette said she was getting a vision that someone was knocking hard on the door—knock, knock, knock!

"I do hear knocking," Pam said with a laugh.

Annette asked, "A loud knocking?"

"Enough so that we think someone is at the door," Pam answered. "For example, I had a daycare here for a couple of years, and one time one of the little boys said, 'Oh, dad is here!' And then I heard a voice. I said, 'Just a minute, let me go see whose dad is here.' I went out to the door and there was no one there! I thought, 'What the heck, and the little boy heard it, too.'"

"Is this house old?" Annette asked.

"It was built in 1985," Pam answered, "but it was built on old farm land."

"It's a new house," Annette said, "but I get the feeling of old."

"The farmhouse used to be over there in the woods," Pam pointed out the window. "And the barn used to be over there."

Annette, now looking out the window, said that she could see the ghost of an old, thin woman out near an old shed on the property. "I almost think she is a Dutch woman. I wonder if any of the original people here were Dutch. I am seeing her with a yoke with two pails. She is getting water, and she is bent over, and she is a very thin, old woman. She looks pretty old to me, but she is a very hard worker. She is not even looking over here, so that tells me that she's a ghost, and she's just doing her thing. We need to cross her over. That's what we do, as they are stuck in their own time, and she is still lugging water. It would be nice for her to know that she could move on. She can cross over and join her loved ones."

Pam told us that she felt that it was not just one person that she was feeling around here, and Annette and Paula were able to validate that there were many ghosts and spirits around her home. Pam said that she is now a believer in "these things," but that at first she tried to explain away everything that happened.

"There have been too many things that cannot be explained. It takes me off-guard sometimes. One time, I was standing here doing dishes, and I was all alone, yet I felt something like a child pull on the back of my shirt. But there was nobody behind me! That probably started happening about two years ago. When it happens, it reminds me of when my kids were little and they would tug at my clothes from behind."

Paula told us that she was getting a strong feeling of a male presence in the home. She also said that she felt there was a woman in the adjoining living room. "She's kind of heavy, and she loves that room, and she loves that chair," Paula said, pointing to a quilt-covered, comfortable-looking chair in the corner.

"That must be my grandmother," Pam said. She explained that they had recently built the addition on the house, and that since they had built it, "It seems like a lot of things have been going on there. We started seeing orbs in our pictures that we've taking in this room, and not just us, but other people have seen orbs in their pictures, too. And the orbs have faces in them!"

"Have you recognized anyone that you know in any of the images?"

Annette asked.

Pam said yes, she believed that she had seen her late brother's face in an orb.

At this point, Annette asked, "Who was Dan, or Daniel, to you?"

Pam sort of gasped, and explained, "Daniel is a child, the son of a good friend of mine, who comes here often."

Annette said that she got this name in connection with Pam's late brother. Annette wondered if it was possible that Pam's brother was a spiritual guide to this boy Daniel.

Pam continued to tell us that Daniel is very important to her because he had two sisters, and that when Jaime was about five years old and Brittany almost one, they were killed in a car accident.

Annette suggested that the tugging Pam sometimes feels could be one of the little girls trying to get her attention. Pam admitted that she has thought she felt the presence of these little girls since moving into this house, and that now that she thinks about it, the accident was not that far away from where she lives now. "It was about twenty years ago that the accident happened." Pam said that she used to take care of the girls.

Annette said, "Just because we don't necessarily see them doesn't mean that they are not here. Spirits and ghosts are certainly around us all the time. They just want to let us know that they are still in our lives."

Pam told us that she has actually never seen a ghost there, but that her daughter Olivia did have an experience which she told us about:

She was watching TV in her bedroom, which used to be the den. It was also my bedroom before I moved it to the upstairs room. Well, she had just shut the TV off, and she was going to go to sleep. She had a little Chihuahua-Pomeranian dog which was in the hallway, where the living room and bathroom meet. The dog started barking, and she opened her eyes. There was someone standing in the doorway. She thought it was her sister, who had for some reason come home.

She thought, "Why is Sissy here?" She looked at the clock, and it was a little after midnight. She thought, "Why is she not saying anything to me? Liv, are you awake?" Then she said the figure looked up toward the ceiling, so she threw the covers back because she was going to get out of bed. Suddenly, she knew something was wrong. She said the minute she started to get up, the person was gone. She came out into the hall, thinking maybe the person had run into the bathroom or something.

Well, this child would not sleep in that bedroom for three weeks after that! It literally made her sick, because there was no explanation. I said to her, "Well, maybe someone was here, and it was a spirit. You don't have to be afraid; it won't hurt you or anything."

She described the spirit as having on a grayish sweatshirt and long hair, and she said, "Mom, I swear to God, I thought it was Sissy."

So then things were quiet for a while, and she was back in her bedroom. I was trying, and trying, and trying to come up with an explanation. I even wondered if it was me, getting up and sleepwalking in the night. She said the girl looked sad and said, "I think something was the matter with her."

Annette said that she was getting a sad feeling from this, too, and that she thought the visitor was indeed a ghost. "I think this girl may have died in a car accident, and is somehow connected to one of your daughters. Maybe the ghost was looking up toward you, because she needed you to help her cross over. She is sad because she is a ghost and she is stuck. I think that she was a classmate, and just because she appeared to one daughter, it may be the other one that she knew. I am just wondering if this young girl came to them looking for help. She may have just picked up your daughter's energy and decided to go with her."

Pam said that there actually was a classmate of her daughter who had died that very night in a car accident, but they didn't think that she was the connection because her daughter didn't really even know her well. "Her picture was in the newspaper, and I said to my daughter, 'Liv, do you think this could be the person you saw?'"

Annette asked, "What did she say?"

Pam replied, "She wouldn't even look at it." Pam said that she thought that maybe her daughter didn't look at it because maybe it would have been too real for her. Annette suggested to Pam that she could speak out loud and address this ghost when she is alone some time, and cross her over herself.

Now Paula spoke up, and asked Pam if anyone has passed whose name starts with an "M."

Pam had to think for a minute, then she said, "Oh my goodness, of course, it's Marguerite!"

She is definitely here, Paula told Pam. Paula told her that Marguerite, Pam's grandmother, is the one who sits in the comfortable chair in the corner, and that she loves the room. We all instantly got goose bumps at that one! Pam laughed and said she didn't realize that she had made a "Grammy seat" when she put the quilt and the comfy pillow in that cozy chair, which she said is just the kind of chair her grandmother would have used in her own home. The quilt on the chair actually had the words, "Faith, Family, and Friends," written on it.

Pam then told us that she had taken a picture one evening in the direction of that chair, and later, when she looked at the picture, she saw that it had a huge red orb in it, just outside of the window, beside that chair. She showed it to us, and it was a very remarkable picture. The very large orb is clearly outside of the glass of the window, and it is dark outside. If you look closely, you can actually make out that there are two figures inside the orb. The way they're positioned, they look like they're looking in the window. Pam insisted that she takes this camera everywhere with her, and the only time there are orbs in her pictures are when the pictures are taken in her own home, especially in this room.

Pam said that she often hears footsteps upstairs: One time I was sitting on the couch. I would go down there to read, and I would fall asleep on the couch. This one time I heard someone come down the stairs and walk into the room and I said, "Honey, I'm just lying down for a few minutes." I thought my husband was looking for me. I opened my eyes and looked, and there was nobody there. So I grabbed my blanket and ran upstairs! That time I was kind of spooked, because I know what I heard.

It doesn't sound like the house is settling—we really do hear footsteps all the time. You know, the dog is not upstairs; no one is up there; there is no explanation. Sometimes at night in my bedroom, I can hear music.

I have never told anyone this before. I can hear music, and one day my daughter told me, "Mom, I always hear music, and sometimes I see this image of someone dancing over my bed."

I had never mentioned to her, and in fact I still haven't, but I also hear music at night. You would think that someone had a radio on, off in the distance. At first when I started hearing it, I thought, well, does Alex have the TV on in his bedroom? I checked and it wasn't on. I just hear music. It is very distinct. It is like old-fashioned music. It is not fast-paced music.

Annette felt that what Pam was experiencing was hearing music from the "other side."

Another entity Annette picked up on was a good-looking man standing in the dining room wearing a suit. The spirit wanted Annette to tell Pam that he "got to wear the suit."

Pam told us that her husband's brother was going to be the best man at their wedding, but the day before the wedding he was killed in a tragic car accident. Pam and her husband had purchased his suit, and had it waiting for him. This beautiful encounter gave Pam and her husband David a lot of peace, as well as faith in Annette's abilities!

"Our light bulbs blow all the time in this place. I've never seen anything like it! Ever. And there was one incident upstairs in my son's room. Lacy, the dog, was sleeping up there and she was standing on Alex's bed and her fur was standing all up, and she was just barking. I went into the room to see what was going on, and the dog jumped off the bed and ran downstairs and into her kennel. I don't know what she was barking at. My son Alex said, 'Mom, she was barking at the wall!' I have never seen a grown dog so scared; she was out of there in a flash."

Annette said that animals can certainly see ghosts and spirits.

Pam said, "Well, that explains it; why the dog was barking in the hall the night my daughter saw the person in her room. The dog's barking made her open her eyes."

Annette and Paula again told Pam that she had many spirits around her, and her house was very active. We all agreed that Pam was blessed to be surrounded by many beautiful spirits of loved ones who have passed.

"Well that's pretty much all there is," Pam said, and we all laughed because we, of course, all felt that, on the contrary, she had quite a bit going on!

*Chapter 40*

# The Mill Agent's House in North Vassalboro

*An article in the local newspaper prompted a visit to a large and very haunted Greek revival-style house on Priest Hill Road. Annette and Paula were intrigued by the article, and invited me along to visit and explore the huge and amazing place, and to hear about the owner's experiences there.*

Ray Breton, of Ray Breton Remodeling and Custom Woodworking, an extremely talented and energetic builder, has renovated the entire place. He lives in one of the six apartments with his Siamese cat named Boo, who, by the way, showed up on his doorstep on Halloween night in 2007. Ray has welcomed many groups of curious people to come and visit the very active home, such as the group "Maine Ghost Hunters." The house has also been featured on the TV program A&E biographies, *My Ghost Story*. People from all over the country have toured the house, and they have shared with Ray their journals and pictures of their visits, which Ray has organized and documented.

The original owner of the 1847 house managed the Vassalboro Woolen Mill. Ray recently purchased the Mill, along with several other buildings in town. He said the Mill is also very rich in paranormal activity.

Ray suggested that we "ground" ourselves on a huge one-hundred-foot-tall burr oak tree in his yard before we entered the house. It is the largest of its kind in the state, he says. Ray believes this "grounding" gets rid of the negative energies people may bring with them. He suggests that visitors also place their hands on this tree on their way out, to clear their energies and hopefully keep ghosts or spirits from following them home. He believes that certain trees such as pines, willows, and oaks, because their roots go deep and intertwine with the earth, are able to take our energies and clear them and ground them into the earth as well.

Ray told us that apartment number one is the most haunted place there, with the ghosts of as many as eighteen children. Ray said he has been told this by more than one psychic medium who has visited. He said the stories of the hauntings go back many years:

I know people that saw him (the main ghost, known as "Captain") forty-five years ago. I have two albums here just full of documentations from everyone who has experienced things here. I could do two more albums with all I've gotten, if I had the time! A lot of different psychics have been here. I've had about fifteen hundred people go through here in just the last year and a half. Things happen around here all the time, it's just ongoing. It's just part of the house. I can sit here and hear footsteps upstairs all the time. I had a group here Friday, and they were up in apartment number one. It's really active up there; that's where a lot of kids (ghosts) are.

There's a ghost there, and she can't handle large crowds, and you know, you get too many people in there and things start to roll across the floor! People come here and expect things, and when things actually happen, they can't handle it! I've lost groups before—they never even made it past midnight! (He laughs) They will bail out of here, run downstairs and out into the parking lot to their car, and they are gone! It's happened twice, and they were younger groups. But most groups will hang in there, like the paranormal groups, and document it. The only two groups I have lost were out of that same room.

Ray's friend, Linda, who is a stained-glass artist and rents a shop in the mill, tells us, "You walk in that door, and it's like you walk into a different time frame. It even has a different smell and feel; it's like two different worlds."

Annette asked where Ray had heard about the eighteen ghost children. He explained:

You know, I could pull out all the different psychics' reports, and in every one of them—some even as much as five years apart—(and they don't know each other) the first thing that comes up is the number eighteen.

A young girl once visited—she lived about a block away from here. This was a couple of years ago, and she was only about fourteen years old. Her mother said she could see "them." I wasn't here when they visited, but they were upstairs, and they went home and wrote down everything. She told me, "Oh my gosh, you had eighteen kids plus!" She saw the Captain, too.

She described him, and I said, "Stay right there," and I went and came back and I opened my book and said, "Is this him?"

And she said "Yes, oh my gosh, that's him!"

There have been paranormal groups that have had a hard time getting information out of here. Their equipment just kept wiping everything out. Their camera would empty, their computers would crash. There's one group that's been here four times, and they've gone away with nothing. It's the only group that this house won't let get out with anything.

Once when they came, they were all upstairs, and one guy went to take a cigarette break outside. They were all big guys, over six feet tall. There were about six of them. One of them looks like the Captain; he's big and he's got the beard. The guy outside looked up on the balcony, and he saw who he thought was his friend. So he waved. Then the other guy walked out near him, and the guy said, "How did you get here so fast? You were just on the balcony!"

The other guy said, "I wasn't on the balcony."

He said, "Yes, you were, you were just there!"

"We were all just in the attic."

Then the guy said, "Oh my gosh!" He was done for the night. I mean, his eyes just glassed over! We showed him the picture of the Captain, and he said that just topped it off!

Now, I know the Captain has a certain wave. So I said, "By the way, did he give you like, one of these little waves?"

And he said, "Oh my gosh!" You could tell that was it for him; he was out of here!

You know, there's not anything really bad or scary here; the kids may just cause a little havoc. You may get pinched, or you may get your hair pulled or moved on top of your head. You may get a lot of poking on your back.

Apartment number six is over a portal. There's an open well underneath it, and so there is a lot of energy coming out of that thing. Very strong energy. It just buzzes. People get a lot of different things, but the thing is, some of the stuff goes home with them. I have no control over it.

One person came here overnight, and he told a joke downstairs, a joke about the Captain, and he (the Captain himself), didn't appreciate it. Well, he went home with that group. He raised havoc with them for a week! I'll tell you what, in the end, they were like, "You've got to leave us alone! This is our place!" The woman said she took a shower, and in the steamy mirror, he wrote the punch line to their joke! She just freaked. She thought at first it was a joke her husband played on her. But when he told her he didn't, that really scared her!

As we listened to Ray's stories, Annette said she could see Ray's grandmother's spirit sitting in a rocking chair beside him. Annette said the grandmother liked that chair, and sat there often. Before we had gone into the house, Annette had felt a sad feeling connected to a woman. She was feeling this sadness strongly at this point in the conversation. Annette asked where apartment three was.

"Right above you," Ray answered.

We went up a winding and steep stairway to another nicely renovated apartment. Annette felt the presence of a ghost who she said was missing her husband. Annette talked to her and told her she could cross over and be with her husband. Annette says this suggestion itself is all it takes sometimes. Paula heard a little click, click sound near me as we talked there. Then Annette saw a little blonde ghost girl with a yellow dress, skipping past us. She was holding a small purse made of soft glitter material with a chain handle. The purse made the click sound that Paula had heard. Ray and Linda asked what her name was. The ghost was playfully teasing Annette, but eventually told her it was Abigail. Ray and Linda seemed familiar with this ghost, and her name, and validated that she was a playful ghost. Annette laughed when she saw her throw up her arms and run quickly out of the room.

Linda told us that the house had a very comforting feeling for her, even with all of the activity. Ray said people are always asking how he can stay in the house; how he can sleep there and so on. He agreed that he also feels very comforted by it, and enjoys the feeling of the house.

Ray said he has found a picture of a man connected to the house many years ago, who is the spitting image of himself. He states that he has seen his own face in the orbs in some of the photos taken in the house. Annette agreed that Ray may be more connected to this house than anyone knows or can understand.

"This is where they do table tipping," Ray said when he showed us the long narrow attic, three stories up. We all asked what table tipping was. Ray explained:

You ask a question that has a "yes" or "no" answer, then the table will start to wobble and spin in one direction for yes and the other for no. You hold your hands over it, but you have to chase it, and sometimes it spins so fast, you can't run fast enough! You actually have to play tag-team with someone, because you'll get sick or dizzy. One time a group had a hard time getting it going, because they didn't ask it right.

I said, "Hey Captain, did you like to give kids rides in the sleigh back in your day?" Well, that table took off so fast and wobbled so hard! Two of them dropped their side of the table. They had never seen a table dance like it did. It was just nuts! I looked over at the two kids with the camera, and I said, "Hey, you two are supposed to be filming this!" They got themselves together, and finally they got some footage. You can see a ten-minute clip on Facebook or the Maine Ghost Hunters website. You'll look at it and think he's pushing that table, but there wasn't a hand on it, and the table was just dancing all over the floor! It was a good session, but it was crazy.

In the attic, Annette felt a presence behind her which she thought was the Captain, though she never saw him. She said the Captain was listening to Ray talking, and he (the Captain) confirmed that "Yeah," it was him.

As we entered another apartment, Annette said she could hear a bunch of children all saying "Hi," "hi," "hi," on and on, in different voices. From there, we went up yet another set of narrow and steep stairs to the servants' quarters. It was a cleanly painted, very old set of rooms, with nicely varnished wood floors. We walked past a large deep-set window, and Ray said that psychics often see a woman sitting there. Paula felt a heaviness in her chest here, and Annette felt the energy of a woman who was very sad here, too. Paula saw a gentleman ghost, who she described as dressed in a suit and with a cane and a droopy left eye.

Ray talked about hearing heavy footsteps walking around the house sometimes. He says he has heard footsteps go right past him and over to and through the cellar door.

As we toured the cellar, which was huge, we also noted the canning jars full of produce that Ray canned. Seeing everything that Ray has created and accomplished here was just as amazing as the house and the paranormal activity. It is hard to believe one man can accomplish that much.

Annette said, "There's something about this room I can't explain. It's something about the word 'secret.'"

"This is the room where the Captain appears most often, and he's very protective of this room," Linda told us.

Annette said she got the word "course" when she entered the room, which was an open section of the old faded brick walls and dirt floor cellar. She felt it had a meaning that referred to a map, like, "You're on the right course."

"I'm getting him smirking; he knows something." Annette continued, "He is showing me this vision, like he's shaking something in his left hand. I hear the jingling. I don't know if it's coins, or if it's keys. I can't see him, but I feel his presence very strongly."

We went into the vacant apartment number one. It had a very formal and grand entrance hallway, with a large winding staircase that went upstairs to three large bedrooms with high ceilings. The living room and kitchen downstairs had large windows and beautiful woodwork, and the living room a marble fireplace. In these unfurnished rooms, toys were lying everywhere on the floor, left by previous visitors who were trying to lure the ghosts of children to appear. It was a little creepy, really.

Down the hall and up a few steps, we entered a little room with a low ceiling, almost like a dollhouse room, painted in yellow. Ray explained, "This is the place where people start to experience things. This is where there is another vortex, and people who come in here get a little lightheaded; a little tipsy. It's something unusual. I mean, visitors won't say anything, but you can see it starting to affect them. The newspaper guy, who was just here, was just standing here with a serious look, and then he said, 'Ray, I have to get out of here.'"

Annette said she felt lightheaded, and I have to admit I also felt the same, though I wondered if it was the power of suggestion.

Ray told us, "There is a slant to the floor, and I have seen this ball roll by itself up the slant, even, when it should be rolling down it. These toy cars here will go back and forth on their own." Annette saw a ghost child who wanted her to throw the ball to him. She also heard voices calling in the distance, as if children were playing hide-and-seek. She said she sensed a lot of children running around. She also sensed a boy holding a car and running it along the wall.

We went back to Ray's apartment, and chatted a little more. Ray showed us more pictures and writings of previous visitors. He has kept very organized documentation of all the activity.

At this point as I was listening, it felt like someone flicked my hair on top of my head. I automatically touched my hair, expecting to feel something there. I almost thought I heard a zing go past my head at the same time. I didn't say anything to anyone then, but later, as I thought about it, and listened to my recording, I remembered Ray had said that this has happened before to his guests. I realized a ghost may have actually flicked my hair! Wow.

Linda asked Annette if she could ask the Captain what his real name was. Annette waited a minute, and said she got the name, "Francois."

Ray said he had heard before that the Captain could speak French. He said that a psychic that visited once asked the Captain to speak in English because she couldn't understand French.

Annette said she was still perplexed because she couldn't see what connection the Captain had to the house, whether he was an owner or the caretaker or what. "I believe he's actually a spirit, though, and not a ghost."

As we were leaving, Annette heard the Captain say in French, "Au Revoir!" Then she could hear several children chanting, "Au Revoir!" "Au Revoir!" "Au Revoir!" —all in different voices!

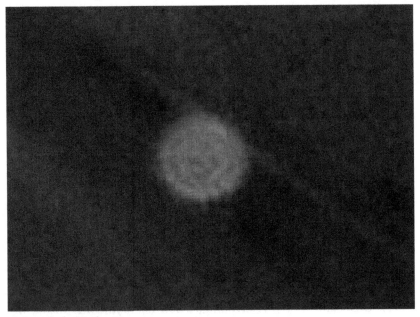

*photograph of orb in the attic*

About a month after this visit, we returned for a nighttime visit—Annette and Paula with their husbands, and I with my very brave Rick. Again we were amazed with Ray and Linda's hospitality and generosity as they showed us around the house again and told us where we could spend the night, or evening, as we dared! We were all excited with anticipation for the night. I was expecting to really see a ghost or to see something move, at least. We brought snacks and drinks, and set up our chairs and sleeping bags, and we were left alone to roam the several vacant apartments, attic, and cellar as we pleased. It was awesome to be there, and there was a very definite atmosphere in the house.

We set up in an upstairs bedroom in apartment number one, and as the others set up their chairs in the empty room, Rick and I laid down our sleeping bags and pillows, and felt foolish that we didn't bring chairs. We discussed what Ray had told us earlier: that he had been talking to someone in town, and he had heard that several children had tragically drowned in the strong current of the mill stream years ago, because they had fallen through the ice there. We chatted awhile, and then Annette saw the small girl with the yellow dress come into the room, right up to where I sat on my sleeping bag.

Annette described this encounter in her journal:

The little girl in the yellow dress wearing the pearl necklace (Abigail) is a spirit, but her brother is still a ghost, and I believe that is why he would not enter the room we were in, even though his sister did, and she beckoned him to come. He stayed in the doorway. (Annette got nineteen children's names, and tried to write them all down.)

The little girl was standing in the doorway, tentatively, holding her hands and playing with her fingers nervously. She is blond, and I believe she is the same one who is named Abigail. Then her brother showed up, and I recognized him because of his dark hair, and she said, "Yeah that's my brother." He was taller than she, and ten years old (she is six), and his name is Michael. She was wearing a pearl necklace, and she was playing with it, and I was thinking, "Wow, that's a pretty nice necklace this little girl is playing with." I knew it wasn't a fake.

So I asked her where she got the necklace, and she said she found it. I said to her that it looked pretty with her yellow dress. The boy was wearing pants with suspenders and I said, "It's okay, you can come in."

Because Cathy was telling a funny story, I said, "It is okay, she's just telling a funny story, you can come in." So the girl walked right in, right up to where Cathy's feet were, but the boy stayed back. She motioned him to come in, but he didn't.

He's like the older and wiser one. Abigail was sitting on the floor near Cathy. "It is summertime," she said, and she said she liked to go swimming.

I said, "Is this your home?"

She said, "Yes, my home."

Then I saw another girl with fancier hair, like golden ringlets in the back. Then I started getting children's names: Mary, Steven, Paul, Benjamin, Vinnie, James, Charles, Marvin, Michael, Susan, Mary Jane, Uree, Haley, another James, Steven, Arnold, Emily, Amy Lou, and Corinne. Nineteen children! All these names just came to me, so I wrote them all down. Maybe they all drowned. Maybe they come because of the vortex— because of the nice energies. I am not sure.

The other boy who I saw in the room across the hallway looked very upset, and I felt I needed to go back sometime and try to communicate with him and ask him his story. Plus, I saw a young girl floating in the water, and Paula saw a boy with no shirt on, with blue in front of him.

After these events Annette wrote about, nothing much happened, so we made a point of not talking, and just listened. We turned all the lights off and stayed quiet for a long time. Nothing. Rick and I felt like we were not so stupid after all, having our sleeping bags to lie on. Soon I heard Rick snoring a little. We heard noises now and then, but we figured it may have been the heat coming on, or other normal house noises. Nothing remarkable happened.

After a little more time passed, we went exploring. We sat in the yellow room with the vortex, and we went into other apartments, and even to the attic. I never would have dared do these things without my psychic friends along to consult with! We had heard that two or three o'clock in the morning tends to be peak time for ghostly activity.

It was really a fun and fantastic night, but uncharacteristically quiet. Ray had said that the night before was quiet also. We were all a little disappointed, and tired, but had a great time in the presence of this awesome house! It's a mystery why a place can be so active some nights and not others. We decided to return for another nighttime visit soon, hopefully a full moon night.

*Chapter 41*

# The Androscoggin House in Wayne

*The historic Androscoggin House was built in the early 1800s by the Bishop family, and was later enlarged and used as an inn by two generations of the Lincoln family, from 1910-1979. In its heyday, it was a very popular spot for vacationers, complete with accommodations for summer guests including many rooms, cabins, a double living room, a porch for dining guests, tennis courts, a park in the woods, and a beach across the street on Androscoggin Lake. The Moon Glow was next to the property and held popular dances weekly.*

Annette, Paula, and I visited with Richard Hollis, owner of the Androscoggin House. Rick told us that his late wife Debra used to insist that she could see a male ghost in the house:

My wife passed away in the year 2002. She was very intuitive about things that were around that I really couldn't see at the time. I will tell you that at first I did not believe in what she was telling me, until I started to see that certain things made sense. There were things that she told me that would later come true about family members and friends.

The story here at this house was that one day Debra was startled because she saw a ghost in our daughter Hannah's bedroom. She didn't feel that he was here to harm Hannah, but Debra got the feeling he had not had a happy life. It was as if something bothered him. Debra was obviously disturbed by the appearance of the ghost, and it bothered her tremendously, and she wanted to find out more about who he was. We talked to our neighbors, who had owned the house previously, and knew a lot of the history. My wife was adamant about finding out who the ghost was, and she believed he had died in this house. Alice was not aware of any stories of anyone who may have died here. But there had been a fire in the attic years ago, when the rooms there were being rented out. A man was sleeping in a room when the fire occurred, and the story is that he got burned and he died later at a hospital.

Annette asked Rick if he knew what year that was, and Rick guessed maybe around the 1950s. Annette said, "I am able to see a ghost who is heavy-set; he is like you described him, not very happy. He kind of gruffly said to me, 'What are you doing here?' So that matches what you are saying, and I don't know who he is yet, but you were describing how your wife saw him as unhappy, and that's how I am seeing him here now. There's something a little unsettling, and he seems to be bad-tempered. So this is what I am picking up from him."

Rick said that he didn't have any sense of anybody being around, and so he doesn't mind the ghost as long as he is not bothering anybody. "And that's how Debra related it to me, that he was not a threat to anybody."

Annette said, "He has his own issues, and he is not related to Rick's family at all, but he does have a connection here, and he may be the man that was burned in the attic room."

Rick confirmed that this man was a boarder, and had no relation to the owners at the time. Annette felt that the ghost was "unsettled" because of what had happened to him. Rick said that Debra had seen this ghost two or three times at the house.

Rick also told us that there was another incident one time when Debra had been standing in the kitchen, and she saw a rocking chair in the corner of her eye rocking by itself. Debra thought it was a guest who was actually in another room at the time. She was so sure that someone was in the rocking chair that she was talking to the person, thinking it was the guest who was actually in the other room. Rick said Debra had also told him that there was another time when she felt someone tap on her shoulder, and there was no one there.

Annette said that she was picking up on another ghost in the house, which appeared to be a young girl. "I'm not sure what her ties are here, but that could have been the rocking chair incident. She is wearing a yellow dress with puffy little sleeves, maybe with a Peter Pan collar. I don't know where she comes from yet, but maybe we can figure that out before we leave today."

"My daughter Haley has a hard time sleeping here at night. She is nineteen years old, and is away at school most of the time these days. She was painting in a room upstairs last summer, painting over some writing on the walls in one of the rooms which was used when it was an inn. There was a name that kept reappearing each time she painted over it, and it scared her, and she ran downstairs to tell me about it. She thought the name was Walter. She had me look at it, too, but we never really decided what we thought was going on. She thought that maybe it was the man that her mother had seen in the house."

Annette said that the man that she was seeing was dressed as if he was from the 1930s or 40s, and that he appeared a little heavy-set and rounded. "He is wearing a muscle kind of shirt; what they called a 'wife beater,' although I hate that term. He is bald on the top of his head. He is definitely here, and I think he is the man who was connected to the fire. I think he was burned all around his face, and I think he would have had issues if he had survived. He would have been an angry man because of his disfiguration, like self-pity. That's the impression he is giving me. It's as if he is not happy with how he died. I don't think he was a very nice man when he was here; he was often moody, and gruff. And yes, I am getting that he was a tenant here. I am going to tell him that he needs to cross over, and go to the other side where his family and loved ones are. He will be much happier and a better person. Sometimes I just say that out loud, and the ghost hears that, and it's up to them whether they cross over or not. So, I'm just putting it out there for this gentleman. I'm getting that his name is Alfred or Albert or Al."

Annette asked Paula if she could see the ghost, and Paula said yes, and that he had just told her he wasn't leaving. Paula said his exact words were, "I've been here for a long time and I ain't going nowhere."

During our visit, this man communicated to Annette that he was here to watch over Rick's daughter Hannah, and that he meant no harm to anyone. He insisted on staying.

Paula said she was able to see Rick's late mother's spirit around him, and told Rick that she was vacuuming, which Paula thought was a way of saying that she is around and wanting to help him in his home. Rick said that his daughter Hannah, who has Down syndrome, has always been obsessed with the vacuum cleaner and vacuuming the house. Perhaps Hannah is able to see or sense her late grandmother taking care of them.

Rick graciously showed us around the very large house with its many, many rooms, which were used long ago by summer visitors in Wayne. Now used mostly for storage, and remaining unused and quiet, the inn part of the house had just a few lingering ghosts. Annette laughed when she saw a ghost—a woman who may have been a maid—and she was down on her hands and knees, looking at us curiously and wondering what we were doing there.

Sometime after I collected this story, Rick and I became friends and we soon fell in love. A couple of years have passed, and I now live very happily with Rick in the Androscoggin House. At first I was uneasy, even scared of the house, since I felt a presence here at times. Now all I feel is a very comforting feeling in this old house.

The first time I spent the night here, I had a dream that there were goats loose and running around in the house. I told Rick about the silly dream, and he was astonished. He told me that at one time Debra had had a couple of pet goats, and had let them run loose in the house for a while. Rick said that she enjoyed telling that story to people to make them laugh.

That really freaked us out for a while, as it seemed like Debra had certainly visited me in a dream. I took it as a good sign from her. Rick said that Debra had communicated to him during a psychic reading a couple of years before we had met, and she had told him that he wouldn't be alone forever. She actually told him through the psychic that she was sending someone to him. I had moved into the house across the street from Rick, so it seemed like there could be something to that story.

Sometimes at night, Rick and I can both hear something like the far-off sound of music playing, as if a radio is on someplace in the house. Could it be music from the Moon Glow?

Mostly though, the house has been very peaceful and quiet for us. Though we are not able to sense the male ghost, Annette and Paula, who visit us frequently, tell us he is still here. We both appreciate the help of the ghost who remains to watch over his daughter Hannah. Who would have guessed when I started collecting ghost stories that I would end up meeting someone so special, and living happily ever after in a haunted house?!

## About the Author

CATHY COOK, born in Eastport, Maine and raised in Winthrop, is currently the town clerk in Wayne, where she lives in the haunted Androscoggin House with her boyfriend Rick. She has two awesome children, Dustin and Jillian. Cathy is a graduate of the University of Maine, with a B.S. Degree in Rehabilitation Services. An avid outdoorswoman and amateur artist, she is also passionate about old houses, antiques, and local history.

Cathy first became acquainted with ghosts at an early age, hanging out in the haunted home of her childhood best friend, "Boo." Ghost stories and other mysterious subjects have always intrigued Cathy, and collecting the stories and writing this book have been a wonderful, life-changing experience! She has met many wonderful people while collecting these stories; many of whom she was meant to meet. She hopes to open minds to the spirit world, which she passionately believes in. This is Cathy's first book
.

## About Annette Parlin

ANNETTE PARLIN is a medium/clairvoyant who lives with her husband Ronal in a 1800s farmhouse in Temple, Maine. "I have always been psychic, ever since I was a little girl. I first saw two spirits when I was about ten years old. They were my guardians in this life, but I didn't know who they were until I was much older. As a child, I experienced many things I did not understand, and it wasn't until I was in my late teens that I met a wonderful psychic who helped me understand what I was experiencing. It was a time when you did not hear too much about the paranormal. I learned to embrace my gifts, and will always be forever grateful to my mentor in helping me grow as a spiritual person.

As I grew older, I felt that I could help people understand more about spirits and ghosts. This is a passion of mine I hold dear. I love being able to walk into a place, be it an old schoolhouse, museum, historical building, a business, or even a private home, and tell people whom and/or what they have for paranormal activities."

Annette Parlin does psychic readings in her home, and also does group readings as well. Anyone who would like a reading can call her at 207-779-6114 or e-mail: psychicannette@hotmail.com

## About Paula

PAULA is very intuitive. She has seen and talked with spirits and ghosts. This all started for her about four years ago after she had two past-life regressions done. Paula has accompanied Cathy and Annette on many ghost adventures, and has shared her experiences for this book. Paula and her husband of thirty-six years live in Wilton.

### *More stories to come...*

If you have a ghost story or other story of paranormal subject that you would like to share, please contact the author at: cathycook1@hotmail.com

**Coming soon...** *Hauntings from Wayne and Beyond...2*

To order copies of this book, please send a check, written to Cathy Cook for $17.95 plus $4.00 for shipping and handling, to:
**Cathy Cook, P.O. Box 376, Wayne, Maine 04284**

# Acknowledgements

I would like to thank everyone (both the living and the nonliving!) who generously contributed their stories for this book.

I'm very grateful for the many courageous storytellers who shared their unusual experiences with me. Their stories were charming and well told, and there were many times when I felt goosebumps, sometimes from head to toe!

Thank you to my friends Betsy Bowen and Robert Stephenson, who not only gave me professional advice, but also gave me the courage to write this book.

Thank you also to my talented and artistic nephew, Daniel Bouthot, who creatively designed the covers of this book.

Very special thanks to medium / clairvoyants Annette and Paula, who accompanied me on many visits and broadened my beliefs, enriched the stories in this book with their interpretations, and became my good friends along the way.

Special thanks to Rick for his encouragement and love always.

Made in the USA
Middletown, DE
30 October 2021